Stephen Becker is the author of ten earlier novels, including *The Chinese Bandit* and *The Last Mandarin*; eleven translations from the French, including Schwarz-Bart's *The Last of the Just*, Malraux's *The Conquerors*, and most recently Dzagoyan's *The Aristotle System*; history, biography, essays, reviews and screenplays. He has given lectures and readings in many countries, and now teaches at the University of Central Florida. He has lived in China, France, and the West Indies.

From the reviews of his previous novels:

'The plot is brilliant, and the style and the dialogue are sharp and elliptical. The book is well above the ordinary thriller, and even a good bit beyond the superior thriller.'
Hilary Bailey, *Guardian*

'A great adventure story, strongly written and a joy to read.'
Desmond Bagley

'The narrative power never lets up. Voluble, bawdy, and zestful, it makes a full and unusual read.'
T. G. Worsley, *Financial Times*

By the same author

STEPHEN BECKER

A Rendezvous
in Haiti

GRAFTON BOOKS

A Division of the Collins Publishing Group

LONDON GLASGOW
TORONTO SYDNEY AUCKLAND

Grafton Books
A Division of the Collins Publishing Group
8 Grafton Street, London W1X 3LA

Published by Grafton Books 1989

First published in Great Britain by
Collins Harvill 1987

ISBN 0-586-20071-1

Printed and bound in Great Britain by
Collins, Glasgow

Set in Melior

To Mary after forty years,
with much love and some astonishment

1

On a parade ground in Flanders two thousand survivors doggedly obeyed bawled orders: boots and rifle butts clashed like iron on the frozen ground. They were two British battalions and one colonial, and their field was bordered by rows of tents, wooden sheds and low ramshackle barracks. Four armoured cars abreast. Autos and motorcycles. A lot full of field pieces. Beyond the artillery, a corral: horses and mules, the shuffle and whinny lost in gusts of winter wind.

Directly before the soldiers, as they came now to parade rest, stood a score or more of Allied officers – a monocled brigadier and his aides, a kepi'd general and his aides, several colonels, the usual junior officers. All but a handful were British, and only two were American, both Marines: Second Lieutenant Robert Alexander McAllister, unblooded, attending his much-decorated Colonel George Barbour.

Frigid air boomed across the field from Belgium; McAllister observed moist eyes and red noses. He observed the sun too – a pale, hostile, silver disc, low in the west behind sullen sheets of cloud.

There was more to notice. Foreign regimental patches, British weapons and decorations and insignia of rank. The third battalion here was motley – a sprinkling of outlandish hats, caps, scarfs, fourragères. And off to the left was a band: trumpets, trombones, a small fat man labouring under a bass drum, a severe, nervous bandmaster. A most unmilitary trumpeter warmed his mouthpiece in the armpit of his greatcoat. A drummer boy was just that: a boy.

The colonel and his lieutenant, latecomers to this war, were on a round of courtesy calls, or, as the colonel phrased it, 'Damn nonsense.' They visited, conferred, learned, made polite murmur, shared tasteless dismal messes. They were welcome, and the invitation to this ceremony had been proffered in hearty solidarity: Americans were fresh and well-fed, pink-cheeked early risers, and the war was as good as over.

The band tore into 'God Save the King', and McAllister saw that the bandmaster lacked a left arm. He inspected the musicians more carefully. One-eyed, a couple of them; a wooden leg; and of all things a missing ear.

A mile to the east, the twin spires of a stone church, perhaps an abbey, dominated the long, pocked slope that had once been farmland.

'This is a grey country,' McAllister murmured to his colonel. 'Paris is grey and the sky is grey and my God sir look at these men. Their souls are grey.'

'Belay that,' Colonel Barbour growled. 'It is January at home too, and these men have fought in the trenches — for three years, some of them. And the Marine Corps does not chatter on parade.'

McAllister shut up. He was more than merely deferential to this colonel, who was not merely a hero with a kaleidoscope of ribbons, but also a diplomat, perhaps a future commandant, or proconsul. Also McAllister was not sure precisely what tone one took with a colonel whose daughter one had fondled.

The music trailed off: a squeak, a thump, silence. The bandmaster smiled fiercely. McAllister murmured, 'And our song?'

Colonel Barbour turned flat blue eyes upon McAllister. 'The British have lost a million men. They're awarding plenty of medals and playing plenty of anthems. All they want from you is courtesy.'

At a sharp, incomprehensible command, the parade snapped to attention. The brigadier stepped forward, and a French general beside him. To one side, a moustachioed major called out names one at a time, and one at a time men marched stiffly front and centre.

The names meant nothing to McAllister. He was large and in rude health; his blood beat hot and vigorous. At a bitter gust he huddled absently against the wind, but quickly he recovered and braced: these men must be honoured. Far up the slope the abbey seemed to sorrow, even to disapprove. And here was a corporal who had led a charge and disabled a machine gun. McAllister

9

had done the same in a field exercise, in North Carolina. This corporal won the Conspicuous Gallantry Medal, and a handshake; and the Croix de Guerre, and two kisses.

McAllister had chosen the military as other men chose medicine or the law, and now a small exaltation welled up. The heroes advanced, were decorated and saluted, returned to the ranks. The wind sang, and stung. A lance corporal. An Indian, in full turban; was this a Sikh? The Distinguished Conduct Medal. McAllister was without decorations; but for the heavy green greatcoat, he would stand revealed, callow among the scarred veterans. The brigadier called another name, the sixth or seventh.

For a long moment no one stirred. Then from the third battalion, the motley battalion, a figure emerged, ambling as much as marching, insolence in his very stride but nothing to define, nothing to rebuke. The man was black-browed, pallid, with a strong nose and thin lips. He stood just under six feet and was of unremarkable build. Some might notice him; no one would remember him but for his brows. He wore no greatcoat; an overseas cap; three previous decorations; and a fourragère. He was a sergeant.

He marched to the generals, faced left, grounded his rifle and came to moderate attention.

The brigadier deferred to the French general, who addressed the men at some length in an accented, wind-blown English. McAllister gathered that the sergeant had served in two of the three Battles of Ypres. Any one Wipers was sufficient butchery for a lifetime. Tens of thousands to buy a quarter-mile dear; tens more to sell it back dearer. Ypres twice! And now the French general awarded a Croix de Guerre and an embrace, and deferred to the brigadier.

The brigadier raised his monocle and stared frankly at this sergeant's face. So did McAllister, who noted the brows, the lax stance, and then sensed more: nothing flowed from the man. This sergeant was not present. He barely acknowledged the brigadier; coatless, he seemed impervious even to the freezing wind, himself a block of ice. Officers whispered. Colonel Barbour and Lieutenant McAllister exchanged a puzzled glance.

The brigadier spoke. McAllister heard 'Passchendaele'. Bloody Passchendaele: useless slaughter, men on both sides blown to bits by their own artillery, and the generals on both sides saying, 'Dirty job.' The brigadier now said, 'Victoria Cross,' and McAllister glanced again at Barbour: the VC was their equivalent of the Medal of Honor, which Barbour had earned in China; the colonel's face was stony and proud.

The brigadier did not pin this one to the blouse: he looped a crimson ribbon about the sergeant's neck, and stepped back, and saluted.

For some moments the sergeant did not stir. It became apparent then that he was in trouble. He swallowed, he twisted his neck, he sucked for air.

At last he coughed. It was at first an unassertive cough, but then it insisted, swelling louder and hoarser. The sergeant gasped, and hawked strenuously, and coughed again, and this time spat up blood.

The brigadier recoiled a step and glanced at his boots.

Blood had smeared the sergeant's chin. He mastered the cough but his chest went on heaving.

The brigadier resumed his rigid attention and his salute. The sergeant only coughed. Now it was a high, strangled cough. He shouldered his arm, faced left coughing and marched back to the ranks coughing, and the sound of his cough carried far, a hoarse irregular shriek surging up the pitted slope towards the abbey as he marched along his rank and turned again, and took his place, and grounded his arm. The brigadier completed his salute sharply, as if the man were still at attention before him. When the convulsion subsided the sergeant stood calm; he seemed to be thinking of something else, to be standing in some other field, among other men. The silence was almost palpable; only when another blast howled down across the parade ground, as if to end the episode, did the major call another name.

Behind the officers the setting sun brightened for a moment, and the battalion cast long shadows, to the slope; to the abbey, McAllister decided; to Germany and Russia and around the world.

* * *

'Christ,' the colonel said later. They had stood retreat with the British, and the French officers; the flags were furled for this night. Barbour and McAllister were crossing the parade ground toward the rickety Hotchkiss touring car lent by the French government to its new ally. 'You want medals, do you? Remember what they cost.'

McAllister could count on a victory medal sooner or later. He would surely see combat; perhaps there would be a special theatre medal. At the moment he was cold and hungry. A soldier approached, walking and not marching, and when he crossed a patch of yellow light between two barracks McAllister saw that it was an enlisted man – other ranks, the British said – and waited, with a pleasure that never failed, for the salute. When the colonel came to a halt McAllister looked again: it was the tubercular sergeant with his Victoria Cross. Americans by tradition saluted the Medal of Honor regardless of rank: the colonel now saluted its equivalent, and so did McAllister.

The sergeant paused, puzzled or careless, and otherwise ignored them. The three men stood quietly in the deepening dusk. McAllister's first impulse was to reprimand the sergeant on behalf of the colonel; his second and better impulse was to silence: a colonel would need no help from a green lieutenant, and a VC no rebukes. Shortly Colonel Barbour, tolerating only so many seconds of indifference, perhaps of insolence, completed his salute, and so did McAllister. The sergeant peered closer, and registered the globe-and-anchor, the silver eagle.

'I'm Colonel Barbour of the United States Marine Corps. This is Lieutenant McAllister.' The sergeant never glanced at McAllister, but the colonel held his attention briefly. 'Congratulations, Sergeant. That's a damn fine row of ribbons, and a couple too many wound stripes. You've fought a hard war.'

The sergeant squinted at the colonel's shadowed features. Their mingled breath steamed in the feeble yellow glow. The sergeant said without heat, 'Fuck your war,' and trudged past them.

The Americans turned to watch this phenomenon out of sight, and when he had melted into the darkness they resumed their march. 'At least he didn't spit on my boots,' the colonel said. 'Too much time in the line, I imagine.'

McAllister only said 'Yes, sir.' He was startled by his colonel's forbearance; he would remember it; rank; noblesse oblige.

'I'm sending you to Paris,' Colonel Barbour said. 'For a week or two only. You'll join General Harbord's brigade at the end of the month. Not staff: you'll take a platoon.'

'It's what I want, sir.' Paris. He would see Caroline. Perhaps the colonel would speak of her now.

'Of course. But let me tell you something. It's not only the British who've lost a million men; the French and the Germans and the Russians too.

14

Colonels pay attention to such numbers. We do not enjoy sacrificing the flower of our manhood et cetera. Your job is not to win medals and lose platoons.'

'I appreciate the advice, sir. But with permission, I don't believe it was necessary. I am not one of your glory hogs.'

'You astonish me.' The wind was slacking. 'Harbord's setting up at Château-Thierry. You know the town?'

'Down on the Marne.'

'Yes. Historical. It's . . . grey.' After a pause the colonel said, 'The Germans are reinforcing all along the line. There will be a hell of a battle this spring, I promise you that.'

'Maybe the last, sir. They tell me we're here to see that it doesn't happen again.'

'It will happen again,' the colonel said. 'I just don't want it to happen to *us*. We may have to run the world yet. Everybody else killing themselves off like lunatics.' The Hotchkiss creaked as they settled in. McAllister spurred the engine to life. 'There's never a last battle,' the colonel said. 'Bit of wisdom: remember it: there's never a last battle. Dim your headlights.'

'Aye aye, sir.'

Night had fallen; the abbey was invisible. Streaks of contraband light flashed from tents and barracks windows. A surge of here and now shook McAllister: he was in France, in this vehicle, in this dream, blood and bone and muscle and gold

15

bar, a cold night, and little yellow lights like cold fires, and white stars pricking out the night now, and a war out there waiting for him.

The whole day had been freakish and foreign – an illusion, a piece of pageantry. The wind singing down from the north, and no sound of shot or shell, and a bizarre ceremony with its Sikhs and Australians and monocles. Generals. A consumptive hero. Crosses and stars and palms and ribbons. A lonely abbey. A one-armed bandmaster.

McAllister saw more of Caroline Barbour than he had dared hope. His brief leave in Paris took him from the Luxembourg gardens (cheap) to Rumpelmayer's (expensive) and from the Invalides (solemn and somehow false) to Sacré Coeur (solemn and somehow true), always in her company. They strolled the famous quais, and crossed the famous bridges. They were happier together than apart; then much happier; then giddy.

He admired what men usually admire: wide-set eyes, straight nose and full lips; he had early noticed her generous bust. Her hair was silky black and her skin silky fair; she mocked his compliments, and told him of her youth as a gawky wallflower blossoming a few times each year for the one male present who could talk horses and look her in the eye from a comfortable eminence. She loved horses. And the adolescent was long gone, matured by travel and war; Caroline was indeed beautiful now, and preserved from vanity by the memory of a lonely silent girl. Her body had at last rounded to match her height, and the miracle of her breasts astounded her every morning – those firm assertions of arrival, those annunciations.

McAllister was lucky: he was a tall amiable young man with curly blond hair matted on his forearms; and his father raised horses. But unlucky too: shortly he was off to Château-Thierry and Harbord's brigade, and by mid-May he and his platoon were one, sharp and ready, and on 6 June 1918, they attacked Belleau Wood and McAllister was riddled by shell fragments. Only four, really, but 'riddled' was what he told Caroline. 'It was the end of the German drive,' he told her. 'They're calling it the Battle of Chemin-des-Dames. They reached the town on May twenty-seventh. We had a machine-gun battalion there and the Wood was just west of town. We went in on June sixth and stopped them cold. And these – funny, it was like being slugged, not stabbed. No pain. I don't even remember a boom.'

'So many of you say that. Nothing hurts till later.'

'We took about eight thousand casualties. I was lucky.'

'So was I.'

He had wangled his way to the IIIème Hôpital Provisoire, where she was a nurse's aide and wore a small red cross. They were not embarrassed by his body and its rude demands; they were not just Bobby and Caroline but soldier and nurse. They had both seen blood and guts and death, and had rid themselves forever of certain reticences.

But not others. Soon they could roam the Tuileries, she strolling and he limping, and once when he had been silent for some time and she said, 'A penny,' he replied, 'That's it. You know I have no money. We're barefoot landed gentry. My father breeds horses, drinks Bourbon and damns Republicans.'

'I hope you're not apologizing.'

'Never. It is no less estimable than doctoring or lawyering or robber barony, and McAllisters have raised horses for four generations – carriage horses and highbred riding horses, and none of your slugs or Percherons. They're obsolete now except on the racetrack. So the old man may go broke,' McAllister mourned, 'but he will not raise hacks for young ladies' riding academies. Excuse me. That was an unintended slur.'

'I've ridden with a number of young ladies,' she said, 'and you are forgiven. Tell me about your mother.'

'A good-looking, round, warm woman who likes to hug my father. They're so happy there's nothing else to say about them. They keep no house servants, for the obvious reason but also because they suffice, the two of them. I'm twenty-eight and they make me blush. And yours?'

'She was tall and elegant, a proper Bostonian with the dry wit they love in New England. My father lived in fear of that wit; God knows he was afraid of nothing else, but she could insult with a gentle smile, and he was always afraid she'd devastate some senator's wife. She never did, of course. She promised me I'd be beautiful, and she dragged me to museums and galleries and concerts, and I miss her terribly. It may seem odd, but she was my closest friend. She died five years ago, just like that, her heart. She taught me when to say "damn" and how to ride astride. I'm sorry, but she left me a lot of money.'

'Then we'll take a rest at the Carrousel,' he said, 'and you can buy me a Dubonnet.' But he was embarrassed. He piled up three saucers while she talked of yachts, and her father's patriotism, and finishing school in Geneva. He talked of the Naval Academy, and guns and drums and wounds. They learned that both had sat a horse before they could walk.

They rambled the Bois de Boulogne too. His leg healed well and grew strong. He was reassigned in August. On the last night he kissed her farewell and again set one gentle hand on the generous bust, and she only said, 'Ah,' and drew back after a moment to lay her own hand on his lips.

He failed her. 'I make seventeen hundred dollars a year,' he said, 'plus ten per cent overseas bonus, and I have to buy my own uniforms.'

'But your quarters allowance is two hundred

and eighty-eight dollars a year,' she said demurely.

'Don't be clever.'

'Our first quarrel,' she said, and kissed him again with fervour, pressing his hand firmly to her, and when he left her hours later he had only time to dash for his dunnage and join his detachment at the Gare de l'Est. But it was indeed a quarrel, the sweet essential quarrel that confirmed love – Christ! the horror of separation, of disagreement, of being less than one! – and it was not easily resolved. The war to end wars ended, and Caroline went quickly home; but he was detained in Europe, and his letters grew defensive, and hers impatient: and when he was repatriated and given at last a good long leave, she had sailed for the peace conference in Paris, where she would hobnob with marshals and ambassadors and prime ministers, and play hostess when her eminent father invited other eminences to grand luncheons and grander dinners, with Filipino messmen to cook and wait upon them.

He applied immediately for European duty, and was sent instead to another war. He wrote to her, cursing the Corps but a stubborn slave to his own choices. Her answer reached him in Port-au-Prince, Haiti: 'If you won't come after me, I'll come after you. *Damn* your pride.'

2

He was First Lieutenant McAllister and he owned three ribbons and was fighting a smaller and balmier war. He was riding miles most days, eating well, sleeping soundly and evading enemy fire; he enjoyed regular leave in Port-au-Prince, a filthy and magical city; and his war eased the ache of Caroline's absence. But it was a queer war, the Marines guerrillas, gendarmes and politicos all at once, the black enemy both friend and foe, the war not a true war but a pacification without peace.

And lately the Marines had been mauled in a number of sharp skirmishes. For almost five years now rebel after rebel, liberator after liberator, had stuck a red feather in his hat and fired away at Marines. The new one was named Martel, and people prayed to him at hidden shrines deep in the forest, and either these clowns were finally learning or some supernatural intelligence was at work. Queer indeed. He was uneasy. Everything he wore was sweatstained or mildewed. October in Haiti was a rotten month, neither winter nor summer, the trade winds slack and sullen, much rain and muggy heat and always the throb of tambours, the Haitian drums that pounded and tapped at them all day and half the night.

One late afternoon he was lying soaked from his campaign hat to his canvas puttees, muddying the dust of a Haitian plain south of Hinche and scattering a ragtag band of poorly armed, half-clad Haitian bandits. He heard a last shot, and saw a distant, fleeing, black figure fall.

'You see him skid?' Private Clancy buffed the sweat from his sunglasses with a red bandanna and expelled a proud spurt of tobacco juice. 'You see that nigger skid?'

Gunnery Sergeant Evans called, 'The captain says we are not to call these coons "niggers". And for Christ's sake pipe down.'

'I just been *shooting*,' Clancy said, and swabbed his upper lip. 'I just *killed* one. They sure as hell know where we are now.' He jacked another cartridge into the chamber.

'Pipe down anyway,' the sergeant said. Evans stood about five eight and weighed about one-ninety, all of it sandy and hard.

McAllister rose, damp and stinking, slung his own rifle and trudged towards the debate.

Clancy said, 'If they didn't hear my goddam gun, they ain't gonna hear a little civilized conversation.'

'You call that weapon a gun again,' Evans said, 'and they'll hear me wrap it around your neck.'

'Mah rahffle,' Clancy mocked him.

Heat shimmered off the baking plain: mirages, sheets of blinding white water that dissolved into sparkles of silver light and then vanished.

'They won't move again,' McAllister said to the sergeant, 'unless they come out for that corpse. I do believe our day's work is done.'

'I think so too. Now ordinarily we would have to wait until this brilliant idea seeped into a lieutenant's head.' The men were securing their weapons and easing closer. 'Lieutenants' heads,' the sergeant explained to them, '*most* lieutenants' heads, are somewhere between bone and stone. You ever see any of that petrified wood from Arizona and out there, Lieutenant?'

'Never did.'

'Sometimes you find a chunk that didn't quite make it, mostly rock but still a little woody like.'

'Sounds about right.'

'Course, if a lieutenant has fought in France, that makes a difference,' Evans said. 'But with the last one I always had to make it feel like his idea. The last one could not count to twenty-one without dropping his pants.'

A drumbeat, a deep hollow boom; then a pattern, pom-pom-boom, pom-pom-boom. Another answered, tap-tap-tap-tap.

'Tambours,' McAllister said. 'Jazz music.'

The drums conversed. Rhythms crossed, urgent. McAllister's fingers danced on his canteen. 'Quitting time.'

'That's what it is,' Evans agreed. 'They do make music. You'd almost think they were human.'

Clancy said, 'Gunny, you might ask the lieuten-

23

ant if that drumming ain't the same as closed up shop yesterday.'

'Feel free to address me directly,' McAllister said.

'Recall,' Evans said. 'Last one, I'd ask the lieutenant if that was recall. The last lieutenant was a salty dog. I mean with the last lieutenant it was all bulkheads and decks and starboard and port.'

'And where is this last lieutenant?'

Evans remembered his manners, and frowned. 'Sorry. He was killed over by Mirebalais.'

'Then respect his memory,' McAllister said. 'Let's go home.'

This afternoon they were completing one of a dozen patrols sent out by the 2nd Marines in October of 1919. After a day's rest they would ride out again, this time on a more merciful mission: to keep a rendezvous with a small Caco village that was tired of war. The Marines would come bearing gifts: extra rations, plugs and small sacks of tobacco, bolts of blue cotton cloth. Today the stick, tomorrow the carrot.

'Caco' was what the rebels called themselves. It was low Spanish for 'thief', but it was also the name of a local red bird, and many of the Caco corpses bore a touch of scarlet: a ribbon around the neck, a red thread twined through a gold earring, a spot of crimson dye on the forehead like a caste mark. They were insurgents and guerrillas but thieves and bandits too, and McAllister was startled by the variety of them. He had expected regiments of identical blacks, but he was fighting everything from villagers in loincloths to light-skinned men in felt hats, dress shirts with no collar, cast-off morning trousers and leather shoes. Martel was a fiery, educated black and no one knew where he might be from day to day; he waged a darting harassing war at the head of a ragtag horde of men and women, and McAllister was tempted to admire him. The Cacos claimed to be patriots, and many carried black-powder rifles from the nineteenth century; and daggers, spears, machetes; some were mounted.

McAllister issued brief orders. His men secured their gear and crooned to their horses. McAllister and Evans walked side by side, and McAllister said, 'When I was a second lieutenant and had not seen combat, gunnery sergeants were next to God.'

Evans grunted: this was good sound doctrine.

'And now I am a first lieutenant, with scars, and I remember what they told me at the Academy: that when I was all grown up sergeants would call me "sir".'

Evans said, 'Aye aye, sir. Sorry, sir. In this goddam country it is like all white men are brothers and we can be careless with our speech. No offence, sir.'

'None taken,' McAllister said. 'It only made me feel small in front of the platoon. That's bad for me and bad for discipline.'

'Sorry, sir. It won't happen again.'

'No,' McAllister said, 'I don't think it will.'

Even in the shade of mahoganies, Haiti baked. The horses had cooled down and watered; men also; no use; they broke a sweat standing still. There was no need for pickets; the trees were sparse here and they could see for miles across the shimmering plain.

In the camp at Hinche there stood one house, headquarters, occupied by Captain Healy and his staff. It was an old house, of stone and mahogany, with a spacious veranda before and, in a small gable, an old-fashioned bull's-eye window. Captain Healy was an Alabamian and said that the smell of slavery lingered – over a century since what these people called emancipation, but still the house reeked of it, the spacious house, the high ceilings and the cool rooms and the phantoms of servants. He knew a plantation house when he saw one; more so when he lived in one. He had never before lived in one. 'White trash,' he liked to reassure his lieutenants.

From the veranda next morning McAllister and Healy surveyed the encampment: shelter-halves precisely aligned, posts vertical and guys taut. The rows stretched the length of a football field, and there was room between them for the clattering Ford truck that brought meat and produce from the town; the truck stood sagging now, steaming and hissing, and in its shade a swarm of children squabbled. The Marines were domestic this morning, policing the camp and sewing buttons on shirts, and sorting laundry for the Haitian men who would call for it and deliver it.

Mules came too, and scabbed local horses, and Haitian vendors offering vegetables, which were refused ('You know what they use for manure'), chickens, which were sometimes purchased, and eggs, which were deemed safe if uncracked and cost one gourde for half a dozen. That was less than a penny each, and eggs were fresh, and beat beans. The cooks kept one of those half dozen as a fee for frying up the other five.

McAllister had discovered an extreme partiality to banana fritters with lime juice, and with Captain Healy was now destroying some three dozen of these. They were served by Lafayette the yardboy. Lafayette was not his real name. His real name was Emilien-zézé or some such. 'This war will never end,' said Healy. The captain's hair started about where his ears finished. And his little blue eyes were usually merry above his potato nose, and most of the day he chewed on Havana cigars that he had free from the US-administered customs. He was wearing britches and a sleeveless white undershirt. He was talkative, and liked to say that a few dozen of him were in charge of finance, customs and police for a country of two million people most of whom were Roman Catholics and also believed that God was a snake. 'You young fellows. War doesn't blunt your appetite. Or maybe it is young love. The colonel's daughter draws nigh.' Healy had not been lucky enough to serve in France, and it was understood that he could therefore take a spoofing tone with McAllister.

'Fritters,' McAllister apologized. 'They are so damn good.'

'It is the French influence. You find a Haitian who knows how to cook, and he's a real chef. The food has improved considerably since the Spanish-American War.' Healy had served in that one; he was restoring the balance.

'Can't imagine what sort of hound's mess you ate back then,' McAllister said. 'I heard we lost more to food poisoning than we did to the Spanish.'

Healy squinted into the past. 'Human meat,' he said lugubriously. 'Sick cows. Decayed hogs. Those Chicago packers made millions. They put the stuff in cans and it was like a hothouse. Every disease known to man and I believe a few that have not yet been classified. We only lost about six boys in combat in that whole war, and they were all Texans and thought we were at war with Mexico. The rest died of overeating, by which I mean eating that garbage at all. I lived on local beans and eggs and yams, and sucked cane for dessert. I was a corporal then and smart.'

'And I was about eight years old,' McAllister drawled. 'Didn't even know I was white.'

'I hope you know it now.'

'You talk as if Virginia wasn't the South.'

'It ain't,' Healy said. 'And anything within fifty

miles of Washington ain't even Virginia. You know they sent mostly southern boys down here because we know how to handle these people. Good Marines got to hate niggers, Jews and all foreigners.'

'I don't hate anyone,' McAllister said.

'Oh Christ, one of those.'

'A matter of family style,' McAllister said. 'The decaying gentry cling to good manners.'

'Just don't be too polite with these Cacos. Kindly bear in mind that they have mutilated dead Marines.'

'I bear that in mind every time I lead a platoon. I also recall Captain Vogel.'

Healy was not pleased. Captain Vogel, serving across the border in San Domingo, had been charged by the Corps with killing and mutilating prisoners. Every couple of wars the Marines turned up some avid collector of body parts. Confined to quarters and awaiting court-martial, he had committed suicide with a small civilian pistol. 'Some things we do not discuss at the table,' Healy said. 'Anyway, you can stay. I need young heroes to do my dirty work. Lafayette! More coffee.'

The lithe, very black yard-boy had almost anticipated him; two steps, and hot Haitian coffee steamed into their cups. Lafayette was perhaps thirty, perhaps fifty. His face was sleek, his eyes were bland. He wore white cotton trousers and a long-sleeved white cotton shirt, and he went barefoot. He was rumoured to have several dozen children in the mountain villages.

The officers sipped in silence. The house faced east to catch what trade winds crossed the plain. Afternoons the veranda was shadowed and they could enjoy beer, rum or absinthe like gentlemen, but now the risen sun scorched.

Captain Healy said, 'You'll move out again tomorrow. Tell your men they have twenty-four hours and they may be out for a week.'

'They know that, sir. I believe we could move out this minute if we had to.'

'Might as well rest the horses, and I suppose the goddam fools will go into town tonight. I do not have the heart to forbid it or set guards on them.'

'They'll be back in time,' McAllister said. 'And while morals is morals, they do fight better after bending a few rules.'

'We can't all be engaged to a colonel's daughter.'

McAllister said, 'I can't afford a ring,' and they set down their cups and withdrew in good order, to consult maps and lists in the cool gloom of the salon.

Next morning the platoon took its leisurely departure after a large breakfast. Captain Healy's career had taught him the military value of reliable and abundant food. 'By God, keep your eyes and ears peeled,' he said. 'Every ford is an ambush, I told you that many a time.'

'No scouts needed on the open plain,'

McAllister said. 'We ride bunched for the first day, maybe two days. Questions?'

A silence. Then Evans: 'No problems, sir. Let's go make the world safe for democracy.'

Captain Healy gurgled and wheezed. 'They just had seven presidents in seven years,' he said. 'If that ain't democracy, what is?'

Laughter broke the tension, and McAllister was glad; he wanted his platoon full of pep and not forebodings. They rode out with a jaunty creak and jingle.

He led his platoon along the edge of the plain, with cover sparse, and the standing untended crops, dwarf yams and stunted maize, and not cane, and little livestock grazing. Tambours reported their progress: the interminable Haitian drums. The beat thumped at them from all directions, and was eerie: the Marines were unassailable but surrounded, while the enemy was assailable but invisible.

For a day and a half they saw not a Caco, but the drums seemed to follow them. They crossed the plain and rode into upland foothills and then into the 'mountains', what the Haitians called mornes, three or four thousand feet and easy enough going, and plenty of open slope. 'Last thing we want is cover,' Gunny Evans explained to Clancy. 'This way we can see a mile.'

'And they can see us.'

'Scares 'em off,' Evans said.

Late in the second day they approached their objective. The village was called Deux Rochers. It stood on a steep hillside and the only serious approach was across a swirling river and through a mile of rain forest. They reconnoitreed for half a mile upstream and downstream of the ford, and then camped and set pickets. In the morning they made plenty of noise, like campers or picnickers, and cooked up another big breakfast, and reconnoitreed again. They would cross on foot and hike up, leaving the horses well out of range with Flanagan's squad. Sergeant Flanagan was a former groom who had joined the Marines when his livery stable became a garage. McAllister liked the man and felt a kinship, and left one of the four Browning Automatic Rifles with him. Reassuring weapons: thank God for the BAR.

The platoon would climb eastward but they would be in rain forest and the sun was not a factor. Six men crossed while the rest of the platoon covered them; when the far bank was secure the platoon followed. McAllister deployed them in two columns with a rifleman at point and another trailing, and flankers out wide, and two laden mules at the centre.

They proceeded with caution — but with safeties *on*, by God. The village had promised peace and loyalty, and requested gifts; and while this rendezvous — negotiated by dubious Haitian gendarmes with inscrutable dark warriors and village elders — exposed the Marines to disastrous betrayal,

Deux Rochers and its people came first. McAllister had seen more than one scampering child or bewildered crone shot to death, the Marine sighting swiftly through brush, or a mist of sweat, or a haze of ground heat, and the victim tumbling.

With luck they would be away in an hour and camped on the plain by sunset. Luck. Around the neck Haitians wore little bags full of luck, ouanga bags they called them, and when McAllister stripped a corpse and opened one of these bags, he found shiny coloured pebbles, petrified lizards' tails, dried hummingbird feathers, a lead bullet, unidentifiable tiny bones, a small wooden crucifix. Luck.

He inhaled the mingled odours of sweat, mule, scrub. His scouts were out wide, his men were veterans. His eyes ached: every bush was – well, an am-bush. Fine time for jokes. He would tell Caroline when she arrived. Fine time to think of Caroline. Still, if he was to die he would like to be thinking of Caroline. She had honoured him with plain talk, a steady eye and an honest blush. A hell of a thing, love.

Not now! His eyes roamed a screen of trash trees. A thrush screeched and fled, a lizard scurried. Easy enough to imagine a skirmish line of Cacos only yards away; to imagine a volley, half a platoon of Marines wiped out in seconds. It never happened. Only at fords. But the Cacos were learning.

A fat black bee buzzed towards the lieutenant like a lazy bullet, and veered away.

Women and children. McAllister had returned from Belleau Wood with vivid memories of anonymous entrails and detached limbs – who was who? friend or foe? Waste, waste. In war was much waste. He had become a stingy killer.

Life was too sweet. Love, he decided, did not improve an officer.

Slowly and in silence the platoon worked uphill, scanning the slopes, noting unconcerned birds and lizards; pausing for long minutes to catch any break in the rhythm of birdcall and rustle.

McAllister's shirt was soaked, his boots were leaden. He was twenty-nine years old and breathing hard. The climb was heavy going for a horse Marine, and when Clancy flung up a hand McAllister was glad of the pause. In the hot silence a cuckoo whistled; when a breeze whispered through the forest, and leaves rustled, it was like the sudden passage of a summer storm.

Evans pushed through the brush. 'Looks good.'

'It does. Quiet but not too quiet. Push on for the village but have your trailer keep a sharp watch behind. Safeties off now, but what I said about women and children still goes. Questions?'

'None, sir.'

And Evans melted into the brush, replaced by Clancy.

'Tell Dugan,' McAllister said. 'Have him pass

34

the word to the rear: sharp watch fore and aft. Then come here to me. You're my runner.'

Clancy said, 'You need a point man, sir.'

'I'm your point man, Clancy. Now do it.'

No one came at them from flank or rear, and quietly they closed in. Like many Haitian villages Deux Rochers was built about a dusty grassy sort of common; a dozen huts of wood and thatch, and as usual one, the houmfort, was outsize, and served as festival hall or voodoo temple. A stream flowed outside the dwellings, doubtless into the river below; in it two boulders loomed like tutelary gods. Livestock ruminated, and noted their arrival: goats, kids – in all seasons, here – a scrub bull and a mangy cow. Chickens scratched and pecked. This was a prosperous village.

In the doorway to the houmfort stood a very old woman, wizened, all in blue cotton.

McAllister saw the crucifix, nailed to the post beside the old woman: Christ on the Cross, wrapped about with a green serpent. He saw paintings on the lintel: an egg, a stick figure, a thundercloud and raindrops. He did what he could with Creole: he used his working French and slurred it. 'B'jou. We have come as planned. Are you the mamaloi? Is there a papaloi or a houngan?'

These were voodoo priests or priestesses; McAllister had never studied this superstition but had acquired a few of its words and ideas.

The woman did not speak. Beside her appeared

a child, a naked boy of perhaps six, all curiosity. McAllister wondered where they buried their dead. Or perhaps a pyre. He had witnessed that: the heap of brush, the smell of burnt meat.

In the forest, birds whistled and chirped; he heard a dog yap, and then he heard the tambors wake, far off, the steady sad beat.

The woman was staring hard at him, as if she could see his past and future. She took the boy by the hand and retreated into the houmfort.

Sergeant Evans said, 'We'd best look, sir.'

'I'll go in with Clancy,' McAllister said. 'You all cover. We'll be going from light to dark and if anyone's waiting for us we're dead.'

'I don't know,' Evans said. 'There's better things in life than dying.'

'Let's do it,' McAllister said, and they walked out of the light and into the dark, leaping quickly once inside, Clancy to the left and McAllister to the right. The temple was less dark than McAllister had feared, and much cooler than he had hoped. He saw a dozen half-naked women and a dozen naked children, huddled against the rear wall, and the old woman in front protecting them all. McAllister said, 'Mamaloi.' He made an effort but found nothing more to say. The old woman only looked, and soon the younger women looked, and then the children. A child giggled. These people had bargained for peace and quiet with Haitian gendarmes, and the Marines might be the first whites they had ever seen.

In a corner, three rifles stacked muzzle to muzzle: ancient Lebels, the first French rifles to use smokeless powder.

The temple brooded at them. McAllister made out a bowl of eggs on an altar, other wooden bowls, some pellets of clay or stone, what might have been a pair of chicken's feet. 'Out,' he said. 'My Christ, out. I'd rather fight.'

'It's the women and children that scare me,' Clancy said.

They dodged outside fast. McAllister called, 'Gunny! These other huts.'

Gunny called, 'A dozen horses, a corral in the woods. Pretty fair horseflesh.'

The other huts contained more women and children.

'That's a break,' Clancy said.

'The hell it is,' McAllister said. 'Where are the men? Livestock. Cassava. I think that's a field of cane across the stream. Those rifles. Two dozen huts, three dozen, and a temple – this is a *town*, that's what. Gunny! You set a perimeter?'

'Doing it now, sir.'

'Hurry up. Clancy, bring on those mules. Fast, now. Have the men stack the goods here in front of the temple.'

Goods: rations and tobacco and bolts of cloth, and eventually four hundred pounds of seed maize. The men worked in silence, running sweat.

And now the Haitian women and children emerged from the temple. Fear and greed and delight struggled openly for their souls. McAllister understood little of what they said but for a moment he felt fatherly and generous. 'Seed!' 'Tobacco!' A young woman quickly unfurled a bolt of red cloth, stripped off her tunic and draped herself in the cotton. A few Marines laughed. 'Never mind the women,' Evans called. 'Watch the woods.'

A few moments more, and the women and children were almost dancing – jiggling and jumping and handling the goods until the mamaloi uttered stern warnings. The children shrieked and made huge white eyes; one approached a wary Evans, and touched the skin of his hand.

'You're a freak, Gunny. Like the two-headed baby at the county fair.'

'Thanks. I still don't like this, Lieutenant.'

'Me neither. We withdraw with extreme caution. Roughly in a circle, right? About fifty yards across. Well spaced. Point, wings, tail. A BAR forward, one right, one left. I don't mind advice, Gunny.'

'That's good enough, sir. One suggestion: when we start across that river, let the forward BAR drop back and cover our ass.'

'By the book. Thanks,' McAllister said. 'Fall back,' he called. 'Clancy, point. Gunny: tell 'em what's what while I say goodbye here.'

To maman he said, 'Where are your men?'

She waved. 'Another village. Vodun.' She gazed

off through the forest, as if she could see the other village.

'The houngans hate us. They agitate the people.'

She did not respond.

'Maman: all this is for peace. Do you understand? If the Cacos come, you will send word. Every month we will visit, with black soldiers to protect you. Next time I want to talk to the men. At the full moon.'

'We had black soldiers once,' she said. 'They ate everything and abused all the women.'

McAllister's heart sank: had the gendarmes been brutal, and then lied? No; she must be speaking of Cacos. 'And your men came home and killed them, and we sent more to kill your men. That is what we want to stop. No more. All right, maman?'

'All right,' she said, almost jolly. 'Such cloth! And scarlet! Now we can all be Cacos!'

McAllister was not sure that he understood this situation.

He breathed easier as they proceeded down the slope, and began to think that they had succeeded in a difficult and perfectly futile mission. They reached the ford. Half of Flanagan's squad was a quarter mile off, with the horses; the other half were in position on the far bank. McAllister's men started across and when about a dozen of them were climbing on to dry land again and another dozen were in the stream, thunder erupted on the right flank.

McAllister bawled, 'Hit the deck! Fire at will!' Davis was the BARman on the left flank, useless for the moment; McAllister saw him whirl and head for the centre, and shouted, 'Davis! Hold your ground!' and shortly over the wowwowwow of rifle fire and the stutter of the other two BARs more thunder rolled, as the enemy opened fire on the left flank and Davis — who had halted in his tracks, whirled again and set up — returned fire.

The men in the stream ducked under and floundered forward. The others were returning fire patiently; McAllister, at the centre, held his fire until he was sure of a clear field, and then opened harassing fire. He glanced up: two mules reproached him. On the far bank Flanagan's men fired steadily. Two scurrying figures detached themselves from the mass of horses: the fourth BAR.

These men had suffered a score of ambushes and reacted without orders. The fourth BAR came into action, sweeping the enemy on McAllister's right flank; the riflemen across the river shifted their fire to the left flank.

The firing diminished. Sixty seconds, or two minutes, and always it seemed an hour. McAllister came to one knee and shouted, 'Anyone hurt?'

'Gunny,' came the answer, and McAllister cursed.

'How bad?'

'Bad.'

'First aid. Where's the wound?'

'Belly.'

'Conscious?'

'No sir.'

An isolated shot on the left flank; an answering burst.

'And Dugan. Jesus Christ, Dugan's dead.'

Silence then, until Clancy called, 'Pursuit, Lieutenant?'

'No! Fall back to the water!' He cupped his hands to shout across the river: 'Shostak! What do you see?' and Shostak called back that the Cacos had vanished, and with every precaution nevertheless McAllister saw his men across. 'Right. Rifles, blankets, stretcher. Four strong men, and for Christ's sake be careful. Where's Dugan?'

He knelt by Dugan, and confirmed the bad news. 'Carry him across. Lash him to his mount.'

He followed, last and still useless: the men had deployed perfectly, each wader finding his spot on the bank and covering those to come; Gunny lay supine on the improvised stretcher of rifles and blankets. Angrily McAllister inspected him. The sergeant was blotched, grey and tan and sandy; his mouth drooped open, his lips slack.

Gunny!

'I don't know how you brought him back alive. He may live. He may be crippled. I would like to hang every Caco in this whole goddam country and cut off their balls.' Captain Healy spat a shred of cigar.

41

'This whole goddam country is not worth his trigger finger. He is the best goddam Marine I ever served with.'

McAllister sat in his own stale weary stink – sweat, the uniform not off him for thirty-six hours while the men bore Evans as if he were new-born, turn and turn about, two by two, cashing in now on the thirty-mile forced marches inflicted by mounted martinets, discovering now even more than in battle why they had been enslaved, berated, driven, punished for a dull button or a bad shave. 'God be good to him,' McAllister said. 'There was not a thing we could have done better. They were dug in and hidden and there was not a sound, not a wisp of smoke or a cough or a smell, to betray them. And they lay hidden for two hours while we crossed, and climbed, and parleyed, and hiked on down the hill and started across. And then they hit us from the right, and in a few seconds they hit us from the left too. If they'd waited another half-minute I might have swung my line and then there really would have been hell to pay. No, I wouldn't have, but it was tempting.'

'Poor Dugan,' Healy said. 'A nineteen-year-old Irish boy from Savannah. He was a fine shot.'

'He was. He and Clancy competed. Clancy is all cut up about it.'

'And I'm all cut up about Gunny,' Healy said. 'We go back a long way. Cuba, Nicaragua.'

'He has a chance.'

'He has a chance to be crippled from the waist down. Let him die, sooner.'

'Is that very Catholic?'

'The Lord works in mysterious ways,' Healy said with venom, 'his wonders to perform.'

'Like educating the Cacos. Captain, we're only one brigade for the whole country and it's their country and they're learning how to fight a war. They're learning from *us*. That Martel is a thinker and a fighter.'

Healy hesitated. 'Those Cacos at Deux Rochers held back,' he said. 'They took present pain for future gain. Niggers don't do that.'

'I thought we weren't calling them niggers,' McAllister said.

'That order came from on high and I passed it along. When I am with my own officers I revert to the ancestral ways.'

'I'm only a little surprised,' McAllister said. 'These people being Catholics.'

'When the McAllisters were grabbing all that free right-of-way and building the railroads, the Healys were their niggers. My turn now. Fair is fair.'

'Don't take it out on me, Captain. We raised horses, not iron horses.' McAllister rose, stiff and sore. 'Like to bathe and shave, Captain.'

Healy waved him away. 'Come back for a drink.'

So later they sat on the veranda again, watching their men keep house, but now they were in shade, and the beer — French, and not bad —

washed away the rotten taste of a disastrous patrol. 'Glad you're back safe, McAllister,' Healy said awkwardly. 'I mean, young love and all. The colonel's daughter on her way. If you'd gone and got yourself killed and made that poor girl cry, I would have felt just awful. And her daddy would've nailed me in grade for the rest of my life.'

At the edges of camp, vendors cried fruit. Not far from the two officers, Lafayette the yard-boy tossed a coconut high, and whacked off the nib as it came down: a moment's wink of setting sun on the blade of the machete and thwack! They saw then that this little fellow was observing the observers, with the barest hint of a smile to come. They stared hard at him, and finally a grin split the Haitian's face like another splash of sunlight.

'He asked me if he could carry my bag tomorrow,' McAllister said.

'Wants to see that plane close up. Listen, you did everything right. Gunny and Dugan were not your fault.'

'Thanks.'

Healy said, 'I still think there's a white Caco. He could be some sort of Spic: does his dirty work, heads for the border and crosses into San Domingo.'

McAllister disagreed. 'You underestimate these people. A hundred years ago they drove the French into the sea.'

'And they haven't done much since. Besides, they had Toussaint back then.'

McAllister shrugged. 'They have Martel now. Tough and smart and they say he makes a rousing speech.'

'Talk and tactics ain't the same,' Healy said. 'Bet you ten we flush out a white man one of these days. One of these days he won't head for the border.'

'Done,' McAllister said. 'A white man makes no sense at all.'

'There's your birdman,' Healy said next day. 'There's our Wyatt.' The Jenny loomed, banked, swooped like a falcon and touched down.

Beside them Lafayette stood entranced, hugging the lieutenant's duffel bag; Healy nudged McAllister, and they shared amusement. 'I'll take that bag,' Healy said sternly.

Lafayette cried, 'Oh, mon capitaine,' and clutched it to him.

The officers laughed, and McAllister reassured the little man with a clap on the shoulder.

The Jenny had turned, and was taxiing towards them.

Lafayette said, 'Ah. Ah mon Dieu.'

Lieutenant Wyatt was a ferocious bantamweight who spoiled for a wrangle every time he vaulted out of the cockpit, which was his real home. His Jenny was the old JN-4, a two-seater biplane with four struts on either side, and when he was aboard, it was as if they had built it around him: he was another element, like the rudder or the stick, a pilot carefully fabricated, with gasoline in his heart and engine oil in his joints.

Then he would grump his way to the ground, where he stood about five foot six, a hundred and thirty pounds wringing wet, and he would glare and puff and bark. The terrestrial leathernecks kept out of his way, as if he possessed the true evil eye. 'Goddam Marine Corps,' he said. 'Goddam Haiti. Supposed to go to France, I was. Could have been an ace. Goddam Germans too full of blood sausage.' He searched about for someone to challenge. Any man in the encampment could have killed him with one punch, but no one would even argue with him. He was their amulet, their guardian angel. 'Christ, that Wyatt,' they said, and shook their heads in supreme approval.

'You know what they got in France?' he asked. '*Airfields.* Even a paved runway sometimes.' His airstrip here was a stretch of plain that baked hard in steady heat and dissolved into sump and bog in overnight rain. 'There is one over by Gonaïves,' he snarled, 'that they got a million slaves to spread a million bushels of gravel on to, and somebody made a fortune, and the goddam gravel shoots up like bullets on takeoff. Tear off your tail!' He scratched furiously at his crotch. 'Not a mechanic in the whole fucking country,' he said.

'You taking off right away?' McAllister had

46

pinned on his ribbons and was a mite embarrassed.

'All right, all right. Goddam sex maniac. I suppose this island going to be full of cocoa-coloured kids in a few months.'

'There's cocoa-coloured grownups running the place right now,' McAllister said. 'Bring me back in three days or so?'

'Any day you like. I once made this run three times between breakfast and bourbon. A goddam taxi, is what. And no white nooky nowhere. Sorry I ever left Burnt Corn.'

'Left *where*?'

'Burnt Corn, Alabama, and no jokes, sonny.'

'Burnt Corn, Alabama. Bet you got a store and everything.'

Healy said, 'We even have railroads.' Beside Wyatt, Healy seemed muscular, even burly.

'Captain! You're not from Burnt Corn?'

'Two from Burnt Corn would be depopulation. No; I'm from Montgomery. Wyatt: how are you?'

'Good enough, Captain. I am going to loop and dump this Yankee out.'

'Yankee!'

'Where you from, then?'

'Virginia.'

'Never heard of it. Captain: you lost a man, I heard.'

'One killed, one wounded.'

'This damn country,' Wyatt said. 'Sorry, Healy.'

Wyatt made a quick farewell, and hustled

47

McAllister aboard. 'Just don't fool with the instruments.' The pilot sang and chattered all the way to Port-au-Prince, but any meaning was lost in the engine's racket and the shrill windstream. McAllister was too busy for talk: to fly was immensely exciting, and below him rose and fell Haiti's verdant hills and valleys, while within him rose and fell his own gorge. He skimmed blue rivers, he terrified whole villages. Faces twitched towards him and Haitians ran for cover in huts or beneath trees, one white-thatched long-legged farmer, stiff as a stork, plunging into a stream and ducking under. Beyond their port wingtip, to the southeast, sullen clouds drifted; to starboard the sky was an immaculate blue. A rude and barbarous land, but beautiful from the air: emerald hills jutting up from the plain, tendrils of black smoke above circular villages; verdigris rivers, or silver, winding to the sea; massing cloud and clear azure sky; and tiny black people, McAllister's brothers and sisters in God's great family, scurrying from a monstrous and incomprehensible wingèd enemy.

3

In cool Kenscoff, a mile up the mountain from
steamy, stinking Port-au-Prince, Caroline Barbour
greeted His Excellency and President-Elect – by
whom elected, no one was certain – and Her
Excellency, and chatted with cabinet ministers
and permanent under-secretaries, doctors and
judges and poets. She was informed that there
was a notable surplus of poets in Haiti and a
notable shortage of plumbers. She accepted champagne. She glanced at the doorway. There were
far too many Marines present who were not Lieutenant McAllister; most were captains and majors.
One was a lieutenant colonel, avuncular – perhaps
presumptuous? ('How is George, that old rascal?'
Caroline: 'The colonel is well, thank you. He's left
Versailles, for the embassy in London.')

She found the Haitians far more intriguing. The
men suffered in bat-wing collars. The wives, of
shades from black of black to warm gold, wore
gowns and scarfs of silk – so hot, but silk! – or
fine lawn or French-milled cottons. Their hair was
curly or wavy or kinky or straight, their noses
were flat or Semitic or Grecian; they conversed in
French and English and Creole.

A Mrs Brundage hovered, pale, American; her

husband maintained the Baptist presence in Port-au-Prince. Mrs Brundage was spare; fortyish; hair in a bun; skirts to the ankle. She whispered from time to time like Gossip in an old play: 'The mulattoes aren't so bad but. Morals simply do not exist but. We do what we can with the New Testament in French but.' Was it worse that Robert was late at all, or that he could not have spared her this dowd? 'Luke works from dawn to dusk,' the woman was saying, 'preaching the Word and doctoring.'

'A doctor?'

'He is a chiropractor.'

'How fascinating,' Caroline said. 'Major! How good to see you!'

Mrs Brundage whispered, 'The major is unmarried. Be careful.'

Colonel Barbour had cabled, PROVERBS 31:29 SEMPER FIDELIS LOVE POP. It was his customary message, twenty times at least in her life of travel, and she loved him for it – the simple reiterated heartfelt unoriginality: 'Many daughters have done virtuously, but thou excellest them all.'

Caroline smiled gently, even mistily, at the woman and said, 'Mrs Brundage, I am a colonel's daughter, and have heard Marines curse. I have been a nurse's aide, and have both placed and removed bedpans. I have seen Paris by night in the company of a Frenchman wearing a beret. Good evening.' She slipped her arm through the major's and they crossed the crowded room.

50

'It seemed time,' he said.

Caroline said, 'She told me, "We were never blessed with children, but we have our Haitians." I'm Caroline Barbour.'

'Of course you are,' said the major. 'And every Marine in the room is jealous of McAllister. How did you meet Mrs Brundage?'

'She was there when I disembarked.'

'You came across from Guantánamo.'

'On the *Catamount*. Captain Tolleson was my father's classmate.'

'You were escorted by ensigns, of course.'

'Three and four at a time, on the bridge. We must have looked like a recruiting poster, or an operetta.'

She wore a dark blue confection of crepe that set off her 'fine shoulders'; yet she felt rather plain, bleached and ordinary, among the Haitian idols. And where was the insufferably casual Lieutenant McAllister, to raise her spirits and restore her bloom?

Shortly she stood beside Colonel Farrell, who asked, 'What did you say to Mrs Brundage?'

'Commonplaces. I'm rather tired of commonplaces. Why do you ask?'

'She has left us. You have accomplished in one night what the Marine Corps could not in three years.' The colonel, who commanded the Marines in Haiti, bowed to a roly-poly black gentleman

51

with long, white, wavy hair. 'Maître! Et comment allez-vous?'

Caroline inclined her head with a smile, and later asked, 'Maître?'

'A lawyer. Nearest thing we have to an attorney general. Ah! Father Scarron! Miss Barbour.'

Caroline shook his hand. 'Caroline Barbour.'

'Jean-Baptiste Scarron.' The black priest bowed over her hand. He was young and cool and athletic, with a faint insolence of manner – perhaps only a steady eye.

'Is it true,' Caroline asked, in English to flatter him, 'that you recognize thirty-two shades of skin?'

There was a break in the swirl of copper and ebony faces, Paris and New York fashions, a wink in the soft blaze of jewellery. His Excellency paused ponderously, a crab's claw in hand; Caroline saw a gleam flash to the surface of his eye, and he inspected her more carefully. She had stolen a moment from them all, in the saffron glow of tropical candlelight, and the priest betrayed an instant's consternation which altered immediately to approval. The colonel stood like a Dresden china dragoon, eyes carefully glazed. He was perhaps more accustomed to commonplaces.

'Indeed, yes,' Scarron assured her. 'Thirty-two for the connoisseur. But at one time, long ago, a hundred and twenty-eight. What is now an art for the eye was once a science for the mathematician. I myself have the honour to be black of black, and if not for the Jesuits of Paris would be digging yams on the mountainside.'

Caroline's pleasure deepened. She missed McAllister even more; if sharing laughter was one of love's joys, laughing alone was one of its sorrows.

'The higher levels of our society are of course mulatto,' Father Scarron continued innocently. 'The infusion of white blood is said to sharpen the wits. His Excellency is living proof.'

For a small and attentive circle, including His Excellency, the priest proceeded to translate his own remarks. Caroline wondered if this was characteristic: was there a Haitian cunning, a Haitian wit? A confident self-mockery was perhaps the mark of a civilized people. How odd: she could recall no self-mockery among the French.

'We have also café au lait, gingerbread, griffe, bronze, copper, creamy and two ivories. Most desirable is Méditerranée.'

'Thirty-two is excessive,' Caroline said. 'In the United States we have only two.'

'That is nothing to boast of,' said the priest.

Smiles congealed.

Caroline's did not: 'Touché. And why do you sound Irish, Father? Your accent should be French.'

'Ah! I was shipped to France as a child, and dragged through church schools and lycées and the Sorbonne; but from that last I took French leave, so to speak, and studied for two years with the Fathers at Dublin University. You must forgive my brogue-an English.'

Colonel Farrell laughed; His Excellency, comprehending or not, laughed in agreement; the evening's flow and glitter and melody resumed. And were accompanied: drums spoke from the darkened hills. Their faint boom pulsed in the scented air, through shadowed archways between fluted white columns, across the candle-lit terrace. From the candles in the salon itself suicidal moths fluttered to the figured cloths of a dozen antique end-tables. The moths were pastel, grey, green, beige. A pale blue specimen bore red rondels, one on each dead wing like some fallen French aircraft.

'By heaven,' Scarron said, 'that is one fine-looking officer. Bigger and taller than I am, and my people were bred for size and strength.'

Caroline glanced quickly at the doorway, astonished at the surge of bliss when she saw McAllister, unutterably handsome in dress whites, a small spray of colours on his left breast. He saw her; she could not look away; and the awful possibility arose of shameful spectacle, public embarrassment, the passionate gaze across a crowded salon. She turned to the priest and asked, 'Am I bright red?'

McAllister was a gentleman first, and only then an officer. He paid his respects to His and Her Excellencies; was presented to a bewildering procession of Haitian dignitaries; and was finally handed along to his colonel. He came to perfect attention, relaxed and shook hands, met a major newly arrived in Haiti, excused himself, and strode – scarcely aware of the brief amused silence – to Caroline Barbour. 'By God,' he said, 'you've brought a priest.'

'By God,' she said, 'you're late.'

'What do we do? May I kiss you?'

'On either cheek,' she said, and when he had done that, and they had clung, she added, 'and quickly on the mouth.'

In time they broke apart.

'We damaged a wheel,' he said. 'I had to help. And what with bathing and changing and being nervous – I couldn't hold the soap. Oh Christ. I would never have believed that any woman could be so beautiful. Does the Father speak English?'

'Lieutenant McAllister, Father Scarron.'

The men shook hands. 'Don't mind me, Lieutenant,' said Scarron. 'Is one of those medals for the gift of the gab?'

'I thought I'd be tongue-tied,' McAllister said, 'so I was going to be the strong silent warrior but I feel like a child. I could hardly button my blouse. I tripped on the staircase.'

'God bless you both,' Scarron said. 'You make me regret my vows.'

McAllister set his hands on her shoulders, and did nothing for many seconds but look into her eyes. He touched her hair, and he leaned forward to kiss her lips again.

'A year,' she said.

'Thirteen months,' he said. 'I almost wrote to . . . release you, but I couldn't do it.'

'Don't be a fool,' she said.

'I do hope you'll excuse me,' Father Scarron said. 'I'll catch you up later and we'll talk politics. If you should require a Catholic ceremony in the next few minutes . . .'

'Stand by,' McAllister said, and when the priest chuckled and bowed and strode away the lieutenant said, 'A Negro. I never talked that way to a Negro in my life. Or a Negro to me.'

'You're not yourself,' Caroline said. 'Our fighting men are not accustomed to well-reared young ladies.'

'That sounds vulgar,' he said.

'To the vulgar all things are vulgar. Are you one of those aggressive service men I read about, maddened by their ordeal?'

'Aggressive! I'm scared to death.'

She considered him. 'I believe you are.'

'I'm just not old enough to go out with girls.' He added less gaily, 'I've had a bad week.'

They held hands for a time, and when they were calm Caroline said, 'Well! We've exchanged the obligatory sighs; how's your war going?'

'Just fine,' he said. 'How's your father's peace going?'

And then it was How was your trip and How is

56

the food and How was Paris when you left and How is Port-au-Prince, and soon they were even able to join the others and participate in civilized conversation.

'Drums, lizards, parrots, huge red spiders, blistering heat, the obdurate Haitian peasant with his spells and his poisons, the primitive Domingan montagnard across the border,' Father Scarron catalogued. 'I pity you Americans even as I wish you gone.'

'It would be the same old mess if we left,' McAllister said. 'Civil war, God knows what. Speak frankly, you said.'

The attorney general sighed agreement. 'It would be Guillaume Sam all over again.'

Caroline asked, 'And who or what was that? I'm new, remember.'

'Came to power in a comic-opera revolt, scarcely able to read and write, and was shortly deposed, when he decimated the aristocracy. He took refuge in the French legation – civilization, after all! Somehow (tiens, somehow!) he was flung bodily over the wall, into the street and the hands of an outraged mob who did what outraged mobs are so often reputed to do but so often fail to do: tore him to pieces.'

'One hears,' Scarron added, 'that they ate his heart raw, there in the street.'

McAllister muttered, 'I'm sorry. I like your country. Is there any middle class at all?'

The attorney general said, 'Me.'

His Excellency enjoyed a rich laugh; they joined him. They were all sipping at vintage Perrier-Jouet in proper glasses.

'And me,' said a handsome coppery woman in low-cut cloth-of-gold. Her glossy black hair lay in ringlets, and between her breasts an emerald glistened. 'If we had a university I'd be a professor of anthropology. As it is I'm only a woman. Society likes me to write at home and publish in Paris.'

'Women are voting in many of our states,' said the colonel. 'It will be national before long.'

'Good God,' Scarron said. 'Elections.'

'You'll have elections,' the colonel said. 'I promise you that.'

'Will they matter?'

Colonel Farrell was taken aback.

'Let me speak frankly again,' Scarron said. 'Last century the flag followed the cross, so I can share the blame. Now it follows the banks. It was good of you to fund our loans, but your reward was railroad concessions and banana plantations and labour for pennies a day. I never hear the Marines mention that. It is always democracy, with the Marines; or "self-government" or "prosperity" or some other indefinable gift. Why not tell the truth?'

'Perhaps because it is not so simple.' This was an olive-brown gentleman with white hair en brosse; the Finance Minister, Caroline believed. She was no stranger to guests of ministerial rank,

58

but tonight's was a grand array, apparently for His Excellency's birthday. 'We owed money to half the countries of Europe – some of them now defunct, by the way – and that was both expensive and undignified. Now we have you, and the difference is notable – we may hope for a functioning sewage system in Port-au-Prince, and perhaps a few decent roads in the countryside.'

Caroline was affable: 'Built by the corvée?'

The attorney general waggled a finger at her: 'The corvée has been abolished. And I thought you were new here?'

Father Scarron said, 'It is remarkable that a young American woman should know anything at all about us.'

The Haitian men bowed. Caroline smiled apologies to the anthropologist.

Scarron went on: 'If not for the corvée, Martel might be on our side. A chief of staff like Toussaint.'

The colonel told her, 'Martel is the rebel leader.'

The attorney general corrected him: 'One of the rebel leaders. A country politician – a warlord, really – called Fleury supplies him with money, and covets the northern provinces.'

'The Cacos,' McAllister said. 'I wrote you about them. Martel refused the corvée, wouldn't do road work so they arrested him.'

'That was worse than a crime,' Scarron said.

'A blunder,' McAllister agreed. 'You knew him?'

'We're of an age. We studied together, with the Fathers, before I left for Europe. He's paid a visit to France himself.'

'A capable man,' said Colonel Farrell. 'A strategist. An orator. A natural leader. He should have been commissioned in the Gendarmerie d'Haiti.'

'I scarcely need remind you,' said Father Scarron at his most icily Hibernian, 'that there are no Haitian officers in the Gendarmerie d'Haiti.'

In time, and in various excellent champagnes, all brut, all seven years old, there were toasts: to His Excellency, the Republic of Haiti, the colonel, the beauteous Miss Barbour, and several long-dead national heroes. Caroline drank cheerfully and told McAllister and Scarron, as they drifted across the terrace and into the gardens, that she was pleasantly tiddly.

'A terrible word,' McAllister said. 'A little girl's word.'

'But that's what I am.' Tambours tapped and boomed from the hills. 'Oleander. That's poisonous.' Tree frogs shrilled, kee-kee-kee. 'And I forget which ear to wear the hibiscus behind. I believe left means available and right not. Or is it the other way around?'

'It depends on the island,' Father Scarron said, 'and is a Pacific custom. Here in Haiti everyone is available.'

'Surely not the clergy,' McAllister said.

'You're a very handsome pair,' Caroline said. 'Both in white. Both in uniform.'

'This is a most unusual evening,' McAllister said to Scarron.

'For me too,' Scarron said.

'I envy you,' McAllister said, 'and I hope the Marines do leave soon. I don't know about banks and corporations. I do know that the Corps wants to clean up, supervise an election, and go home.'

'Home to the plantation, I believe.'

'My men are dying,' McAllister said.

'Yes; my apologies. And why do you envy me?'

'Your future. You may even be president of this country some day. I don't say all priests are selfless and honest; but it's a place to look.'

'Good Lord. Most of our presidents are poisoned or blown up.'

'That's why I'm here,' McAllister said.

Lieutenant McAllister and Miss Barbour made their farewells to various Excellencies and Honourables, to the colonel and assorted majors, to the attorney general and the anthropologist, and to Father Scarron. They descended stone steps and crossed a dark gravel drive by the light of torches in tall cressets. Distant drums still beat. In the drive coachmen sat like wax figures, glowing yet colourless in the licking torchlight; sat like well-trained circus tigers. McAllister handed Caroline into a fiacre; the night was dry and the roof was folded down, so they sat prim and proper, only holding hands. 'A long day for you,' he said. 'All those ensigns.'

'A remarkably handsome wardroom,' she assured him.

'Swabbies,' he said. 'I wish we were at the hotel. I'd like very much to put my arms around you.'

'I think I'd like that too,' she said.

And they arrived not at Olofsson's, which was full of Marines, but at the Grand Hôtel de Paris et de Port-au-Prince, which was small and clean and quiet, and they climbed the wooden stairs together, and crossed the broad threshold together, and walked arm-in-arm to the balcony to look out over the city. They kissed, tentatively and then with passion, and they stood embraced. The tambours followed them even here, and in some black alley a child wailed. McAllister drew back to look carefully at his lady's face.

'Don't you dare say goodnight.'

'You're exhausted. I'm a brute.'

'No, you're not. I'd call you homely but honest.'

'That's me,' he said.

'You're still not sure.'

He released her. 'I make two thousand dollars a year plus two hundred overseas bonus.'

'But your quarters allowance has risen to four hundred and thirty-two dollars,' she said.

'I told you not to be clever. Anyway I *still* have to buy my own uniforms. How do you like my dress whites?'

'Unbearably handsome.'

'Ten seconds ago I was homely. You're as confused as I am.'

'I'm a bit confused about our tomorrow,' she said, and retrieved him, 'but I am not the least confused about tonight.'

On the Wednesday – what was Wednesday? Here the days flowed, merged; perhaps Sunday would orient them, churchbells – they joined Father Scarron to attend a public function. 'By all means wear your medals,' the priest had said. 'Be resplendent. Don't come to Saint Rita's; I'll meet you at your hotel.' Now they were strolling the boulevard in the general direction of the Champ-de-Mars, Caroline and Scarron in white, McAllister in khaki; Caroline carried a parasol and wore a wide-brimmed straw hat. 'It is the first school to be dedicated in over a year. Le tout-Port-au-Prince will be there. A chic woman will lose an earring. Sleek men will murmur assignations. Elegant polyglots will sweat like pigs. There will be no refreshments and in the end we will drift out of the courtyard and go our ways.'

McAllister grumbled, 'Why drag us along?'

'A demonstration of progress. Also, you paid for it. And your uniform will create goodwill among our upper crust, whom you are defending from soulless revolutionaries.'

'You're making fun of everyone,' Caroline said.

'Yes. I'm sorry. I spend too much time in the company of God. It leads to snobbery.'

'Is your Martel soulless?'

'Not a bad question. Without a soul he would not rebel; but to rebel, one must sell one's soul. He has sold his to that Fleury, up north.'

'How very Gallic: a French Lucifer. What colour is Martel, of the thirty-two?'

'Quite black, and his people are on the whole far blacker than the aristos here. Yet Fleury, his principal support, the Engels to his Marx, is an ivoire, a backwoods populist sugar magnate who yearns for the purest democracy. I believe shade is a matter of indifference to Martel; a useful weapon now, but he has promised himself and others to abolish those silly distinctions.'

'Not Lucifer, but Robespierre.'

'No, not Robespierre either: Charlemagne. He was named – though I am not sure by whom – Charlemagne Masséna Martel. Martel was a great king, and Charlemagne was his grandson, and Masséna was one of Napoleon's favourite marshals.'

'He was the Prince d'Essling,' McAllister told them, 'and Napoleon said he was the Revolution's favourite son.'

'Le fils chéri de la . . . wasn't it victory's favourite son?'

'Well, I don't recall now,' McAllister said.

'I'm impressed,' Caroline said. 'You may ask me to dinner.'

They had left the boulevard and now entered a flowered courtyard through a gateway in a stone wall higher than a man. In the courtyard buzzed a crowd of starchy, formal appearance, and at its deep end stood the school. There was an improvised stage, and before it stood some forty folding chairs of the kind McAllister associated with tent shows and Fundamentalist corroborees. Behind the school there seemed to be another street: roosters crowed, dogs barked. 'Many of these guests are politicians,' Father Scarron said, 'but the level of manners will be high. There will be no assassinations.'

Caroline said, 'The scents are wonderful.' Many of the women wore jewels and flowers. McAllister bobbed bows left and right. Men consulted in grave metropolitan French, with many a 'formidable' and many an 'évidemment'. A handsome, bespectacled, black-haired woman in a blue linen suit greeted them; Caroline recognized the anthropologist, whose name now proved to be, rather oddly, Langlais. Caroline asked, 'I suppose this is a parochial school?'

'Well, they all are, you see.' Madame Langlais seemed apologetic.

Not so Scarron, who said, 'And why not?'

McAllister laughed, 'Catholic or voodoo?'

Madame Langlais said, 'I wouldn't joke about vodun.'

'Yes, I'm sorry, you're right,' McAllister said. 'I tell my own men not to joke about it. Some of them say they've seen files of zombies.'

'Nothing to do with vodun,' Madame Langlais

said briskly. 'Your men saw them in farm country?'

'I suppose so, yes,' McAllister said.

'What you call zombies are catatonic hebe-phrenics, touched in the head and very often kept on a doped diet. Malnutrition, cretinism, superstition – and a traditional source of slave labour. Horrible. Vodun, on the other hand, is a religion. A real religion.'

'Indeed,' said Scarron.

'Farm country,' Caroline said. 'It sounds so peaceful.'

'It's not dull,' McAllister said.

Scarron asked, 'When must you go back?'

'Day after tomorrow,' McAllister said. 'It's just patrols.'

'And while you enjoy the countryside,' Caroline said, 'I languish in my room.'

'I shall show you the big city,' Father Scarron said.

The school was a white wooden shed with a corrugated iron roof also painted white. The shed was perhaps thirty feet by twenty, and the play-ground or courtyard about thirty feet by fifty: here the children would kick a ball, beat one another, scream and shout and sulk. Within the shed, Father Scarron explained, they would glance for a few minutes a day at some outlandish text, surely French in origin. 'Some day we'll teach in Creole. For now they will learn, or be exposed to, the life of Toussaint, the highlights of the French Revolution, the alphabet and some arithmetic. They will hear a few of La Fontaine's fables and will be reminded again and again that Haiti is the only country in the world to have revolted, abolished slavery and expelled the former masters.'

There was of course no electricity for this school, but that would arrange itself quite soon.

There was of course no plumbing but that too would arrange itself quite soon.

There were no books but that was irrelevant because there were no students.

'Any Haitian who can afford unemployed ambulatory children can afford the lycée,' Father Scarron said. 'But the Americans paid for this public school, and we Haitians are a polite people – cette fameuse politesse française, after all – so it has been constructed and advertised and every effort will be made to seat at these small desks deserving Haitians between the ages of six and twelve. And one of them will some day be a cabinet minister and it will all have been worth it.'

The audience straggled to its wooden chairs and applauded politely at the mention of France, the United States, and the Haitian government. The school was described. It was to be observed that the east and west walls were mainly shutters, so that the presence or absence, indeed the very velocity, of the trade winds could be taken advantage of. A plaque would in time be erected, commemorating the generosity of the American people, who were the friends and benefactors of all the world now that war had been abolished.

'It is that sort of function,' Scarron murmured. 'Everything is in the passive voice. Oh dear God,' he went on.

They followed his gaze, towards the gate. A beggar was entering, almost unnoticed. Caroline took McAllister's arm.

The beggar was not old, but toothless, apparently, and one-eyed, and lacked a left foot.

An Excellency was stressing the French heritage of this great country.

The beggar was wearing a tattered tunic and hopping on one wooden crutch. What added zest to the occasion was the beggar's sex and prominent breasts and, for the moment, the audience's sublime unawareness.

Caroline experienced a rush of affection for McAllister. She tried to thank him – for existing, for being there with her – but it was a wry smile.

The woolly beast advanced. She plucked at a sleeve. A muffled cry wavered through the hot courtyard. Her mossy hair was crowned with lint, leaves, a green insect.

His Excellency was praising Henri-Christophe, Napoleon when young, and Woodrow Wilson.

The beggar continued along the outside row of chairs. Her eye gleamed. The occupants of those chairs shrank, fiercely attentive to the orator. A chorus of locusts chirred from beyond the wall. The breeze had dropped. The beggar approached the first row, and attempted to pass between the speaker and the spoken to. Gasps were uttered. His Excellency saw her in detail then, and faltered. The beggar hopped from dignitary to dignitary.

His Excellency was equal to the occasion. He did not quiver in fury, nor did his voice rise. At his simple gesture a squad of police sprang up, as if he were Jason sowing dragon's teeth. Almost before they converged, the beggar raised her free arm defensively and hopped once or twice towards the gate. Then they were upon her, two raising her off the ground while another clubbed at her and three or four more shielded sensitive observers from the necessary indelicacy. The audience returned its attention to His Excellency. Within seconds the beggar had vanished, translated to some other state of being.

The ceremony ended at last, in a buzz of mutual congratulation. Greetings and farewells were exchanged. A few Haitians caught McAllister's eye, bowed and grimaced; they were apologizing for the brief display of bad taste. Le tout-Port-au-Prince, chatting and chuckling, sauntered from the schoolyard like churchgoers dismissed. A man in gold pince-nez kicked a wooden crutch beneath the schoolhouse in passing. The anthropologist made her adieux. Father Scarron walked beside Caroline and McAllister; it was obvious that he wanted to speak and could find nothing to say.

Caroline was wondering what sort of school this

was without a jakes, or at least a hole in the ground where 'deserving Haitians between the ages of six and twelve' could faire pipi.

Nights were muggy, and the electric power ebbed and flowed, died, flickered to life; most of the city lived without it, and bulbs and fans were playthings of the aristocracy. Caroline and Bobby made slick love, and caressed each other with rubbing alcohol and sat quietly in the dark on the small jutting balcony. They held hands and enjoyed the street sounds: cocks crowing at midnight, shrieks of laughter, the shuffle and clop of donkeys. 'You could extend your leave,' she said. 'After all, a colonel's daughter.'

'That's just why I can't. And nobody knows it better than a colonel's daughter.'

'Yes. But how will I live? Two whole weeks. And I don't like people shooting at you. Has it been rough?'

'Some. When you lose men. The worst is, it doesn't seem to do much good. This is a big country for one brigade. We're lucky the Haitians squabble. There's at least half a dozen ambitious rebels and some of them hate one another more than they hate us. You have no idea. Family feuds. Provincial warlords. Rich idealists like that Fleury. I shouldn't complain. If they got together we'd be in real trouble.'

'Let's go inside. I waited a long time for you.'

'You won't believe this,' he said, 'but I waited

longer for you. I was never brave enough for fleshpots or rich enough for grand bordellos.'

'A poor virgin, but mine own,' she said.

'Well,' he said.

'That's right. I don't want to know. Farm girls and haystacks. Inbred half-witted southern belles.'

'I like you jealous.'

'You were less smug before your promotion. Oh, Robert, yes.'

Before he returned to Hinche they decided to marry when his Haitian tour was over; money be damned. Simply to look at him, awake, asleep, naked, clothed, stopped her breath. And she was immensely flattered by the change she worked in him: with her he seemed to live in another air, one of perpetual and imbecile bliss, of stunned witless amazement at his own good fortune. She never said, 'Don't let yourself be killed.' He was a serving officer, and even in a war that was not a war, with no brass bands and no headlines, his work was more than a duty: it defined his life and gave him purpose, and she would not have him other. After all, that work had brought them together. He would not marry her now, only to send her away; nor would he leave her a young widow. Very well: what could she do but wait? Meanwhile he would have seventy-two hours every fortnight. It would have to suffice. Perhaps she could not do as virtuously as Pop wanted, but she would excel them all in fidelity.

4

Louis Paul Blanchard did not make for the border. San Domingo was of no interest: more Marines, strutting Spanish bandits, and no old friends. He had disembarked in San Domingo almost two years earlier, after a voyage of three weeks from Lisbon on a stinking rusty tramp, a sugar boat returning to San Domingo city half in ballast. He learned that raw sugar, pulped sugar, stank; not merely an odour but a nauseating odour, and the runoff was called *bagasse* and if all those ladies with their pinkie up could smell it once they would never again say, 'Two, please.'

He knew no Spanish, and soon boarded a coaster for Port-au-Prince; in Haiti his talents might be useful. His cabin-mate was a business-man, poisoner and pimp, Haitian-Jamaican, who talked forever about himself and Haiti in a bastard French that was not quite Creole. Blanchard did not like his cabin-mate and lost him upon arrival, but was grateful for the introduction to Haitian ways.

He then spent three bizarre days on a new planet, after which he felt very much at home. Port-au-Prince embraced him. He came ashore amid the mingled aromas of hides and fish, on the dock, and blossoms, great banks of them halfway up the hill. Men and women smiled. Working men wore bald heads or narrow hedges of kinky black hair down the middle of the scalp. Working women wore kerchiefs. The bosses wore straw hats. These bosses were lighter in colour and fanned themselves often with their hats. Some had wavy hair, glossy in the sunlight. People said hello as he passed; a woman would stop beating her child to say B'jou.

Blanchard did not give a damn whether these people lived or died in poverty or wealth, but they were not measuring him, either for a swindle or for a coffin, and he appreciated that. He rarely spoke; he listened; when he did speak, it was good country French and soon a fair Creole. He was warm, and coughed less. The bread here was like French bread. He could not believe the prices. He was carrying eighty-five British pounds, some of it blood money, some stolen from corpses and some won at cards, and he reckoned it would last him a year and a half if he never earned another farthing.

Soon he found women, and he found cockfights, and he found the kind of work he was trained to do. He was twenty-four years old, and he decided he would remain, until fate directed him elsewhere, in this land of cheap rum and cheap life. He could not understand why these people laughed so much and so happily, but perhaps time would teach him.

* * *

So he did not make for the border after the ambush at Deux Rochers. He sat apart for a time and cleaned his weapons. He endured the fit of coughing that followed high emotion. He returned to his men for a cup of rum; he praised them. He enjoyed a grand dinner of roast goat, rice and beans, with pawpaw for dessert, and his men were exhilarated and soon blind drunk on clairin. They had earned their binge. He watched their teeth flash in the firelight and wondered what he might accomplish if faction ever ended, if the Haitians ever set aside their squabbles – families! colour lines! blood feuds! – and gathered under his command. Let Martel be king, emperor, god, and let that Fleury be philosopher or treasurer or whatever, but let Blanchard be commander in chief. Today his men had fought with intelligence and discipline. But he would never be commander in chief and his men would, on another day, fight like cowardly squabbling bandits.

In the morning he dispatched a runner with a verbal report to Martel and added that he was taking a week or two of leave. He made for Port-au-Prince, pushing along the hillsides, picking his way, hungry and pausing often for yams or cassava, or to hear the drums. On the ridges he would be noticeable, and in the valleys were villages and farms; the memory of roast goat made his mouth water, but he settled for a river fish. There was plenty of forage for his mount. Blanchard was now twenty-six, and owned four hundred and forty dollars in gold plus all that was on his and his horse's backs. In a scabbard at his saddle he carried a Lee Enfield carbine; in a holster at his belt, a revolver, the Colt .45 of 1917; in a sheath hung a long slaughtering knife and in a pocket nestled a smaller clasp knife. He carried ammunition in his belt and in bandoliers. He liked money and wanted more. In other respects he considered himself prosperous. The sun and rain fell soft upon him; what he ate tasted good, and he bathed in pure streams.

He called his horse Sammy because the French liked that name for animals. He had once been fond of a dog called Sammy. He had no idea what the horse had been called by its former owner, a huge blustering Caco chief who had believed that shouting and caracoling would scare Blanchard to death. The saddle was old, and did not count in Blanchard's financial estimates. It might be a French saddle from long ago, a hundred years or more, that had lain unused in a shop or attic or tack barn for decades. The silver was tarnished but he was polishing it bit by bit, and the leather had sprung back nicely, sucking in bean oil and gleaming with new health. Or Spanish. He did think some about that: it might be Spanish. A high pommel. He was not sure that the French used high pommels in the old days.

The taste of anger was still strong, but it was a habitual taste. For many years now the rage had been working in him. That was a phrase he had acquired somewhere, a book or a magazine or maybe a preacher: the rage was working in him. He turned his mind to Cleo and immediately cheered up. He did not smile, but he patted Sammy. Cleo's was an establishment of quality, with a wooden floor, walls and a true roof. The house was set upon four stone footings. Cleo kept four women and kept them strictly.

He entered the city by night, walking Sammy through familiar alleys, and was challenged only once: a shadow emerged from shadows, and Blanchard saw the faint gleam of a blade. He asked, 'Ou v'lay balle dans lobwi?' and the shadow fled down a lane. A handy phrase, condensing much foolish conversation: 'Would you like a bullet in the belly-button?' Blanchard moved along amid the odours he remembered, wood-smoke and grease, filth and poverty, dried fish; but also an unquenchable waft of forest and blossom, slipping down these leeward hillsides on the confused trade winds.

Cleo's house marked the edge of the true city, with buildings of stone and wood rather than huts of plank, withe, sheet metal and oil drum. Within the wall and behind the house stood a shed; he led Sammy there, and pumped water into the trough. He heard motion in the house, and Cleo's voice, sharp: 'Qui moon?'

'C'est moins,' he said. 'Ouvri p'r moins. I'm hungry.' The Creole was musical and reminiscent on his tongue, crooning and purring as if it were his cradle talk.

Cleo showed open pleasure: 'Oh my Blanchard! Welcome home!' She pronounced his name the French way, and he liked that; and if her love was purchased, the friendship in her voice was free. 'Eggs and bread?'

'And coffee.'

'I have tripes too.'

'No jokes before sunrise.'

He heard her issue commands, heard other voices. He was pleased. He was home. He hung Sammy's tack and gathered his bedroll and weapons, and climbed the three wooden steps to his town house.

He woke with the sun high: no shadows in Cleo's little room. He slipped into a pair of loose cotton trousers and padded out to the jakes, and then to the pump. This pump was why the fence: thieves respected Cleo and kept their distance, but ground water was a valuable commodity, and women would have come a kilometre with buckets. Gift of a grateful politician, the pump was. So much was, here: life from the grateful rich, death from the ungrateful.

Clean and awake, he turned to Sammy. Cleo had been at work: a truss of hay, and the horse munching at a generous heap of it, and water in the trough. He entered the house and greeted the girls: four, each with her own cubicle, and he never bothered with names. They changed. 'Bread and coffee,' he said. 'Is there confiture? And where is Cleo?'

'Yes, and she is at the market.'

With windows open at the east and west, the little breeze took heart, and almost whistled. Blanchard stood before the pier glass. This was Cleo's purchase, and no gift. The four women swept and scrubbed, washed the earthenware cups and plates and also washed themselves, frequently, and on gala nights they wore short tunics of bright hue, and spent long moments before the pier glass applying cosmetics and perfume. Cleo's was a modern establishment, with a cache: floorboards, the rifle oiled in its scabbard, the pistol oiled and holstered, the slaughtering knife, accessories. Blanchard did not favour weapons in Port-au-Prince: only the clasp knife. Old-fashioned courtesy wrought miracles in Haiti, town or country. He had considered a very small pistol, a .32 perhaps, but had decided against it. Never had he quarrelled in Port-au-Prince. And if he should? When he was not working he did not kill. He was a professional.

Cleo was also a professional, and he responded to that: a madam of skills and graces, and a canny, reliable friend. She was perhaps forty, a woman of oval face and sinewy body. She and Blanchard could be calm together. They could talk. Haitians tended to be indirect, but Cleo was straightforward with Blanchard. Among the men anything more complicated than the purchase of a small tot of rum required silences, appraisals, grumbles, half promises, second visits. This wearied Blanchard, who had learned to appreciate plain blunt talk and to despise roundaboutation. Cleo would not say, 'There is a spot of mildew on the matting,' only to arrive at her point some exchanges later; she would simply say, 'We have a small leak in the roof. Can you plug it and paint it?' The roof was of galvanized metal and the heat played hell with it; but for a year now Blanchard had mended it patiently. He had stolen paint from the Marines, and a set of tools. These were his contributions to the household. He was young to be head of a family.

Cleo returned, a fine dark woman of the colour they called griffe, her hair kinky and her nose aquiline. 'Some Frenchman a century ago,' she liked to say. 'An aristo.' Today she brought millet, dried fish, herbs and spices, ten eggs and a sack of fruit, mango and papaya and local apples.

'You spent all my money,' he said.

'Half a dollar,' she said, 'including this,' and she revealed a bottle of clairin. The label proclaimed 'Chevalier,' so the bottle had once contained hair tonic, perhaps a hundred litres of rum ago. A smug white man with a copious head of shining black hair was still visible, though perhaps the hair shone dimmer these days. 'Party tonight. Ça va?'

'Sure,' he said, 'but I think I'll just waste the day.'

She kissed him. 'Not altogether, serpent blanc.'

The party was nothing special: a Haitian had been hired by an American bank, and was treating two of his friends. Blanchard holed up in Cleo's room. He had joined a party once and only once: the Haitians dried up and drank in silence, smiling every few minutes and asking him how he liked Haiti, and how long he planned to stay, and how he had acquired such fluent Creole. Cleo had driven him out of the house; he had taken it with good humour and strolled down to Boniface's for the cocking.

Tonight he tried to think but the revelry was shrill. The host had been hired not merely as a sweeper but as janitor of janitors. He was to receive eighty gourdes each week, and – this he confided in a shrill, exulting cry – there would surely be small change on the floor, in corners and cracks. His cronies jubilated. Blanchard could picture the scene. The house illuminated by coconut lamps, a hollow half-shell with a wick floating on an inch of oil; shadows on the whitewashed walls; the girls' gowns vanishing, and only the panties left, Cleo's notion of grand luxe, silk panties, and the girls' breasts brushing the men's faces as Cleo made friendly murmur and served out clairin. Then a sophisticate, perhaps the new bank clerk, would suggest a song, and Clarisse, that was her name, plump and pretty, would sit in a corner on a cushion and chant a rhythmic plaintive country tune.

A lizard scuttled across Blanchard's ceiling. Sammy whickered; Blanchard rolled to the window; nothing. He waited; nothing.

He slept until Cleo joined him, and he cried out at the taste of her, and they coupled, and laughed, and coupled again, and swore they were lucky, and slept snuggling.

'So,' he said next morning, 'if there isn't yet a price on my head, there will be. Maybe just a little medal for the man who does me in.'

'Le Caco blanc,' she said. 'So! My man will have a price on his head.'

'Le Caco blanc. I hope they aren't cheap about it.'

'A white man can do much that a black man cannot.'

'Not for long,' he said. 'The black men fought like lions this time.'

'They come here, you know.'

'Who comes here?'

'A Caco, now and then.'

He mulled this. It occurred to him for the first time that Cleo might one day betray him. He did not enjoy the notion but all things were possible. 'Any Marines?'

'Never.'

Blanchard was amused. For a moment he saw

that lieutenant plain: patriotic and heroic, the sugar of the earth. 'Like to be a colonel and command a regiment,' he said. 'Surprise the Marines. Drive them into the sea. Saw one the other day I wanted to kill with my own two hands.' He was bewildered again by a surge of emotion, and wiped his mouth with the back of his hand.

'A colonel?'

'No. A lieutenant.' He frowned. 'Saw him before somewhere. Here in town, maybe.'

'Another aristo,' Cleo said. 'One of them has a young woman who has chased him here.'

Blanchard said, 'Haw! You mean a white girl?'

'In Port-au-Prince,' Cleo said. 'Everyone talks of her. You know how we love our gossip.'

'Your gossip scares me,' Blanchard said. 'You know how I love my privacy.'

Occasionally Blanchard considered taking ship and sailing to some other war. Stinking rusty tramps, like the one he knew, plied the Caribbean and the South American coast, and smoked into Port-au-Prince or Gonaïves every few days. But he dismissed the idea. He would not skip out of Haiti. He would not leave his friend Cleo. He would not leave French for Spanish or Portuguese. And he would not abandon Sammy. Who could be trusted to care for Sammy?

Saturday night was Cleo's big-money night. Blanchard talked to Sammy for a while, and fed him a handful of cane, and when lamps pricked out the dark city and he could feel a fever rise from the alleys and shacks, he ambled off towards Chez Boniface. He had discovered the arena many months back by asking the first Haitian he saw wearing shoes, 'B'jou, monsieur. Dites-donc, pour les concours de coqs?' The Haitian bowed, as if to an authority, a connoisseur of cocking, and answered in what sounded to Blanchard like Parisian French, and poetical at that ('Just past a clump of frangipani aswarm with noble green larvae' was almost too much for the soldier). They shook hands; they bowed again.

The walk to Chez Boniface was Blanchard's favourite promenade. He could remember snowy streets (and did, in this darker world), the dazzle of lamps, the cloud of his own breath; and endless fields and dense forest; rabbit scut and deer scut bounding from muddy trails; hay in summer, the ice breaking up in spring; but here the night was denser and the scents were richer, and the constellations seemed new. He strolled through a dense garden of murmuring aromatic Haitians; the streets were thronged.

Chez Boniface was a spacious circular fair-weather arena with a wooden shack, about two feet off the ground on four sturdy legs, midway along the eastern curve. This shack was Boniface's residence and it was roofed. The entrance was simply a break in the circle from a boulevard to the north, and fifty feet to the west, along the scruffy grass ring, or gaguerre, was the bar. This consisted of barrels, bottles, planks and cups, plus one or two cheerful bartenders. The circle consisted of a tall palisade of branches, reeds, slats, poles, planks and other improvisations. During the rains Boniface retired to his garçonnière with a keg of rum and his fiancée of the moment; the bar closed down; and the gaguerre dissolved to mud. In fair weather every night was amateur night, but Saturday nights were serious. A good cock was to Haiti what a good bull was to Spain.

When in session, Chez Boniface was the noisiest stadium in Port-au-Prince. There were plenty more gaguerres in the city, some operating all day and taking entry fees from, as Boniface said, 'anybody with a canary'. Country boys would come twenty miles with a handsome stud chanticleer bred for the pot and not the pit: they would fight him and bet their last gourde on him and wander disconsolately home with the corpse. The poor Haitian rube! Blanchard was almost sorry for them, with their future coq au vin and their dreams of winning a hundred gourdes.

Boniface himself was a prosperous man and looked it – a jovial, opportunistic old pirate, eyes roving but not shifty. Blanchard almost liked him. As they chatted, Boniface would observe, scan, inspect; but when Blanchard spoke of a price or a stake, Boniface's eyes aimed into the soldier's like the double barrels of a shotgun, and their intensity was like a small blast. 'V'là Gérald,' he would say.

'Triste, li. Ti-Noël made off with his Juliette.' He heard everything and talked freely about everything – or so it seemed. God only knew what secrets he kept. Blanchard had never heard a word about himself that could be traced to big round Boniface. But he had kept the fat man's secret: Boniface was a Caco of talent and conviction, who served as contact, conduit, spy, behind his gossip's disguise. 'Lots of clap at Monique's place,' he would tell a crowd. 'Stay out of there a while. V'là c'cochon de Roger. He goosed his black last week, with a nail. Highly illegal but nothing could be proved. The bird flew into a rage, you figure it, and demolished Blot's zinga.' A zinga was a grey or a speckled grey.

Boniface was rarely without a bottle in his hand; he nipped parsimoniously but with regularity. He was one of those fortunates who grow round and rich in a limited area, and are quite close to absolutely happy. (Blanchard had once known a baker of similar attainments.) This terrain was Boniface's. The establishment was honest, and was frequented by Haitians of high estate and low, who never saw Boniface truckle to a rich mulatto or play the lord with a landless peasant down to his last gourde.

When Blanchard arrived, one main had already been fought. He slipped through the entrance, dropped a gourde into a waiting hand, and sidled along the outer wall towards the bar. The obligatory drink was clairin, with or without rainwater.

Whiskey was a foreign decoction of exorbitant price. Gin was known as a Dutch poison. Beer was available: local beer was hogwash and foreign beer an extravagance. But rum! Clairin! The island was awash in the stuff.

The handlers, in fact, sprayed their cocks with an airy mouthful of rum just before the match. Ruffled, the indignant birds would raise their hackles and flap their wings and strut complaining until they had worked themselves into a murderous mood. The handlers were entitled to ullage – one for the cock and one for themselves. They would further infuriate the contestants by immobilizing them while a specialist filed the spurs that made them lethal. Once the spurs were filed, there was no turning back; all bets were on, and scratches were forfeits.

There were peckers and slashers. Peckers took a while to do their work, like boxers jabbing a victim to death over ten rounds. Slashers leapt high and came down hard, the spurs flashing and sometimes blinding an enemy eye or penetrating the enemy brain; they were like fighters with a vicious hook in either hand, who could end matters early.

Blanchard ordered clairin à l'eau. This was handed him in a capacious wooden cup. He then toured the gaguerre, and heard talk more appropriate to racing: 'That black is a slow starter but comes on strong at the finish,' or 'The red has won his last three times out; hardly worth a bet at tonight's odds,' or 'The brown doesn't look like much but I know his trainer. If the price is right I go for ten.' The air was full of admonitions, curses, greetings and cigar smoke. Most of the men wore the familiar white or blue cotton trousers and loose shirt; many were barefoot; but a few wore collarless dress shirts or imported pants. The women seemed to be whores; he saw none of the moon élégan', no Near Eastern empresses or Queens of Sheba. It was a good noisy cheerful black crowd. He was at home and almost happy in this mob of rumbustious Haitians.

The betting was moderate. There were a few professional bookmakers but mainly it was man-to-man. Bettors were offering as little as one gourde. The highest sum called in Blanchard's presence was fifty. He would bet twenty – a dollar, give or take a few cents. He had come for the entertainment and the company, and his profession had taught him the dangers of gambling.

As usual, every time he saw a flash of scarlet in someone's get-up his mind said 'Caco'. But that was habit, not fear. This evening he had no enemies. He was cheering impartially for two peckers. The flow of blood was impressive. It mingled with remembered flows, faint confused images from his several pasts. The red had lost an eye, but the remaining orb gleamed like a ruby as he attacked, attacked, hopped sideways and attacked again. It was, as cockfights go, classic. If either bird had flapped his way into the air and come down with a well-placed spur, the match would have ended; but they were peckers.

He gulped clairin. He was thirsty and sober. 'Vas-y le rouge!' he shouted. Startled faces gleamed at him. 'Messieurs-dames,' he said, and hoisted his cup in general greeting.

'Soir, le blanc,' a voice called.

'Tout le monde!' Blanchard responded. The crowd was growing shrill, its nighttime roar swelling. Men stamped and cursed. The red was wearing down his foe. That was a waste. Suppose he won? A one-eyed cock would never fight again anyway, but boil up nicely with onions. Simmer for some hours, please. These were tough little birds. The loser was reddish too, more orange, and he stabbed back gamely, but he was being forced to give ground and circle. It was not that he lacked heart; only that he was smaller. His handlers were not permitted to touch him except to keep him within the ring. Each time he hoped to flee, they herded him back to his doom.

Now the orange was hard-pressed, and the pit was all feathers and shouts. Along the palisade, lanterns flickered from the sheer force of sound. The red closed in hard and the din was fierce, but by God the orange gave them their gourde's worth: fought back standing, fought back beaten to a sit, down on his tail; braced and strained himself into one more flurry and went over on his tailfeathers again, doomed and battling, and at the last second he fetched red a roundhouse swipe with one spur and the lone ruby eye dimmed. They died like that, the red with his beak in the orange and a spur in his brain, and the cheering was fierce. Men and women roared and yodelled and applauded and clacked their wooden cups together in rhythm, and in the corner by Boniface's little dwelling a tambour rataplanned, and a deafening hooraw went up for Mince Serpen' and Cheche Crachat, or Skinny Snake and Dry Spit, who were the birds embraced in death, and for Achille and Charlot, who were the owners embraced in life. All bets were off, and the camaraderie was like warm mist.

A quartet of handlers were setting out another main. The murmur of Creole soothed Blanchard again, like some country melody from another century. The handlers examined spurs, their own bird's and the other's; they ruffled feathers, they blew a fine spray of rum. Noise mounted. These were another red and a zinga. Blanchard sized them up. 'Le zinga!' he called. 'Qui moon ba deux?'

The chatter checked: who was this white fool, asking two to one?

'Imbécile!' someone called. 'These are great birds! Five gourdes! Evens!'

'Even money,' Blanchard agreed, and the crowd pressed in, and the clairin was sweet. The handlers were ready, the cry went up, the birds circled, fluttered and attacked. They sparred, broke. The zinga was a slasher and bided his time. The red seemed a hybrid, slashing and pecking both. When the birds paused for rest, the handlers gathered them in. They were set again; Blanchard saw the handler jab, and the red lunged forward in a frantic flurry and pecked blood from the zinga's neck, and then slashed. Blanchard shouted, 'Foul! Coup-bas!' Furious, he leapt into the pit and took up the zinga. For that instant he saw and heard nothing; only knew that he had been fouled.

A handler in a red headband came straight for him. The man was café-au-lait and moustachioed. Blanchard now saw that he was a runt, but his blade was eight inches and bright. Blanchard shielded himself with the cock and shouted, 'Ça va, ça va!' while he groped for his own knife. In the back of his mind he cursed himself: this was neither paid work nor a cause. The handler cursed and spat. Blanchard told himself, just two country boys arguing, but he knew how wrong that was.

There was a ring of them suddenly and no wall behind him and no way out. Blades wrote flashing illegible messages. Blanchard forwent his knife; he crouched and raised open hands like a wrestler; the zinga flapped to earth. Blanchard talked fast. 'You goosed that red. You goosed him hard.'

Another handler dashed into the circle to reclaim the bird, and dodged away. The crowd cheered, and Blanchard heard: this was better than a cockfight. Two to one on the black. No bet on the blanc. The ring was all knives and teeth, edging closer. Blanchard could only stand still.

Boniface came waddling, cheery and curious, a bottle dangling in one hand. 'Tiens,' he said. Then he cried out, 'Ohé, merde! Shut up, all of you!'

They did shut up. 'Ten times a night one protests the handling,' he went on. 'What the devil is all this fuss?'

'Not to Marius,' a voice called. 'Marius is an honest man.' The crowd agreed in a peevish mutter.

'You see, setting-on is legal,' Boniface said to Blanchard. 'Perhaps it is done differently here.'

'Setting on! He damn near disembowelled that red with a railway spike.'

'Such talk,' Boniface said.

'Look in his pocket,' Blanchard said.

'We do not look in pockets here,' Boniface said. 'As well, don't you think?'

Blanchard drew a deep breath and stood tall. He sniffed tobacco smoke. The ring of men was still waving knives at him, and their faces were not angry, but sullen and scornful. The moustachioed handler muttered to Boniface, whose brows rose.

Blanchard suppressed a cough. He choked, wheezed, swallowed and hawked vigorously. He tried to spit politely.

'Calm yourself,' Boniface said.

Blanchard said, 'I'm calm. You calm these others.'

'Any man has a right to debate,' Boniface told him, 'but you are the only blanc in the gaguerre. It makes a difference.'

'I have been the only blanc at more than one cockfight.'

'But consider: you are an outsider and you lay down the law! Perhaps the goosing was to throw a match, and the throwing was to settle a family feud; perhaps lives have been saved. Or would have been, without your interruption.'

Blanchard did not speak. The crowd too was silent now; not hostile, only curious. A cock fluttered, and screeched rudely. The mist of clairin and smoke, the flickering lamps, the silver blade; Blanchard stood alone, on this other planet. Finally he said, 'Yes. I understand,' and to Marius, 'Pardon, mon vieux, pardon.'

Boniface said, 'V'là, Marius. The blanc apologizes and knows better now.'

Marius grumbled.

'More heart, more heart,' Boniface insisted. 'A handshake, now.'

They complied: a loose West Indian handshake. The crowd murmured. A man shouted, 'And the birds? And my wager?'

'Well done, Marius,' Boniface said, and Marius nodded, neutral, no harm done and the quarrel ended. He turned back to the business of the evening.

Boniface spoke quietly. 'Now, mon cher. Shall we go to my loge? It seems to me we might profit by a conversation.' He raised his voice: 'On with the main! Drink up!'

These welcome instructions were acknowledged by happy shouts, while Blanchard and Boniface strolled back to the loge.

They sat on the floor of the small wooden shack, backs to the walls, and sipped at clairin. 'We heard about Deux Rochers,' Boniface said. 'It must have been a glorious moment.'

'It was,' Blanchard said. For some moments they listened to the boisterous crowd, the shrieks of encouragement and groans of dismay. It was not the walls that vexed Blanchard, but the ceiling: he missed the cold remote stars, the endless free fetches of nothing. 'It was. There are not many of them.' He had no friends; Boniface and Martel were as close to him as any men – not close at all; Boniface enjoyed the ruses and schemes, while Martel . . . He tried to recall the friends of his youth, and all he could evoke was the bare house, woodsmoke, desolation, the river and ponds iced solid and the sides of pork like marble in the shed.

'We know the Marines,' Boniface said. 'We can deal with the enemy.'

'We!' This fat civilian. 'We could drive them into the sea,' Blanchard said, 'with better organization and real discipline. If I could shoot a few cowards. Good God, what has he got for an army?

Bandits! Superstitious idiots! Women! Greedy Domingans! He calls himself a general – do you know that he has a soft heart? Fleury can be a lot crueler. That's another thing – Fleury hates me. Or so I hear. You know about that?'

'I do know. He hates most blancs. But faction is a worse problem. Batraville in the south, Savoie in the north – too many generals, too many kings. So you took leave without permission?'

Blanchard scoffed. 'And I won a victory without help. And I haven't been paid for some time. I want some action,' he said, and now there was passion in his low voice. 'I want money, I want an army, I'm tired of leading a mob and I'm tired of taking orders.'

Boniface dipped into a shirt pocket and came up with a packet of cigarettes. He offered them. The cigarette papers were a golden tan in lamplight. Blanchard raised the cigarette in salute and thanks.

Blanchard knew he would cough. He did cough, and when they saw the blood on the back of his hand Boniface said, 'Eh, eh. It will pass. The hills of Haiti are like heaven.'

'It will pass,' Blanchard lied, and waved smoke. He tugged at his kerchief and wiped his hand. 'I came on business. Why can't we just parley outside?'

Boniface said, 'It would hardly do to talk business in the gaguerre. Tonight, for example, we have two corporals of the gendarmerie, betting

94

their month's pay. Not to mention a few of Batra-ville's people. A country of miracles. One never knows who is who. If God himself came to walk among us he would look like a beggar or a docker. You fell into good luck, picking that quarrel. Marius is a known Caco; therefore you are not, but just another blanc. What's this business you came on?'

'I'm going to take a white hostage. I need help.'

'A white hostage!' Boniface was a man who liked to smile; he took his time, and relished the moment.

Blanchard nodded.

'And you need help.'

'Only to take her. I'm too conspicuous.'

'That will be easy,' Boniface said. 'When you make servants of a whole race, they have free run of you – my men will go where they want and as long as they seem to be sweeping or scrubbing no one will see them. And afterwards?'

'A mule cart, three or four good men.'

'To?'

'To Martel. I don't like the man but he's the only boss I have.'

'A hostage will keep the Marines in camp, is that it?'

'Or bring an interesting ransom. I like money. So does Martel. It buys arms.'

'Where is he?'

Blanchard shook his head.

'This was his idea?'

95

'Haw!' Blanchard spewed contempt. 'Never! He won't even talk to me. I'm a real soldier and a blanc and he owes me money.'

Boniface said, 'You underestimate him. Be careful.'

Blanchard shrugged. 'Listen, I need good men. To take her is nothing, but once we have her, every bandit in Haiti will say, "Why didn't I think of that?" and come after her. I can't fight my way through fifty outlaws.'

'I can find you talented thugs,' Boniface said, 'but not to trust.'

'Then I won't trust them.' Blanchard said.

'They'll want cash.'

'They'll have it.'

'You did say "her".'

'A colonel's daughter.'

'Oh my God,' Boniface bubbled. 'Oh holy blue. Colonel Barbour's daughter.'

'You know about her.'

'All of Port-au-Prince knows about her. Some lieutenant's sweetheart.'

'Young love,' said Blanchard. 'I knew her father, in Europe. He saluted me once.'

'You go too far,' Boniface said. 'Never lie to me, not even in jest.' He filled his lungs with the rich sweet smoke and said, 'Tiens,' and sat pensive.

Blanchard was uneasy in the pause: this fat bastard was conniving, already two jumps ahead of him. He held forth his cup, and Boniface ceased scheming, and poured him another tot. They chatted calmly then, about times and places, potions and poisons. Then his host showed him out, a hand on his shoulder to steer him through the larking crowd, and as he left the gaguerre he heard Boniface announce, 'So much for that one. No more blancs in this gaguerre, is what I say.'

Blanchard finally smiled. The son of a bitch had no morals at all.

5

At Hinche they greeted McAllister with the ritual
raillery. Evans was still alive, conscious, on a
warship with doctors, could move his legs: Captain Healy was exuberant. Lieutenant Dillingham
was back from a long patrol; he was McAllister's
friend, a rugged, voluble roughneck much liked
for his fund of blue stories and his affection for
alcohol. He was also fearless and deplored notions
of permanent peace. 'I am happy to see you here,'
he told McAllister. 'You may now lead patrols
while I visit Port-au-Prince and see this colonel's
daughter for myself. I plan to take her to dinner
and tell her the story about the orange horse.'

'The ones on the left,' McAllister said, 'are forks.
The knives and spoons will be on the other side.'

Dillingham cursed him joyfully. The three officers were lounging on the veranda, dimly aware
of the drums, and Lafayette the yard-boy was
bustling, bottles of beer and rounds of coconut
meat. He had taught them to wrap a bottle in a
wet bandanna; the least breeze cooled it right
down.

Healy said, 'Lafayette: you want to make some
more money?'

With a tight sly grin Lafayette said, 'Capitaine
v'lay femme.'

'No, no femme. Moi v'lay see a zombie.'

Lafayette's grin vanished. He stood silent, small, black, empty.

'Come back from the dead,' Dillingham said. 'Do you believe that?'

'No, I don't,' Healy said. 'I don't believe in zombies and I'll tell you why. Christ brought Lazarus back from the dead, correct? And Christ was the son of God himself, correct? And Christ only did it that one time, correct? Well, if you think some country nigger's better'n Christ, you're no Catholic, is all I can say.'

'I'm not,' McAllister and Dillingham said in chorus.

'You Catholic, Lafayette?'

'Oui, Capitaine. Moins Catholique.' Lafayette crossed himself.

'Okay, no zombies. You can go now.' Lafayette glided away immediately and Healy went on, 'You know what that sumbitch does?'

'What now?'

'Why, he's practically American. I inspected his quarters. He has a shelter-half and a gardener's shed. And they are both full of full bottles.'

'*Full* bottles?'

'Right. Full of local white rum, beside which the lightning of Jehovah is as balm and the kick of a mule like the caress of a virgin. Old beer bottles and wine bottles, and fat green bottles you can't see through, and old hair-tonic bottles and square bottles like the apothecary. And you know how he filled those bottles?'

'You're going to tell us,' McAllister said. This was the best time of day — still light, but the air freshening and the sun settling comfortably into the green hills.

'Well, he took an old story, a local legend, and he decided to *do* it. I tell you, gentlemen, for every swindle there is a new audience — a new clientele, you might say — in each generation. That is a scientifically verified principle which accounts for the survival of the British Crown and the Republican Party. What our boy Lafayette does is this. He takes a bottle and half fills it with water. He then hies himself to a grog shop. You know them?'

'Seen one or two,' Dillingham said. 'A wooden booth with three sides, and in the middle a barrel of rum.'

'The more tony establishments,' said Healy, 'are roofed over. Anyway this clairin has to be sold fast or it dissolves the barrel. So Lafayette asks the man to top off his bottle of rum. And the barkeep pops a funnel into Lafayette's beer bottle or whatever, and sluices a half-bottle of his private stock into it.

'Naturally before paying out good money Lafayette allows himself a small sip, just to verify, you might say; and then he sputters and curses and throws a fit and shouts 'Rotgut!'

'And he pours back the half-bottle. If he has to,

he snatches up the funnel himself and does it. And if the barkeep starts to hoot and holler, Lafayette even gives him back an ounce or so extra. I imagine there follow a few imaginative and injurious remarks on both sides, but Lafayette is already on his way off the premises, headed for the next distillery.'

Dillingham said, 'By God. After three times he'd have seven-eighths rum.'

'And after four, fifteen-sixteenths, which is a proportion legally sufficient to warrant cattle pure-bred. And this stuff is clear as a mountain spring and young as the dawn. Three tots of it will flush the liver and lights for a week.'

'It is a corrosive broth,' Dillingham confirmed. 'I'm not even sure red blood cells can survive in it.'

'The men don't seem to pay much attention to the rules,' McAllister said. 'Rum and whores. Talk about tradition.'

'Boys will be boys,' Healy said, 'and the Corps is famous for improvising in unforeseen circumstances, where theory proves inadequate. Lafayette sells this poison by the bottle or the half-bottle or the pony and he is making big money, and if I tried to stop him I would have a mutiny on my hands.'

'Or if you tried to clean out the women in Hinche,' McAllister said.

'You are not to be thinking about sluts,' Healy said.

'That poor colonel's daughter,' Dillingham said. 'In the clutch of a rapist. You been to those cribs, Mac?'

'I only know what Gunny Evans told me.'

'God bless the man,' Healy said. 'Here's to him,' and they hoisted three beer bottles, and Healy added viciously, 'and a fatal clap to that son-of-a-bitching rebel Martel.'

Gunny Evans had deplored those shacks outside Hinche, the poor goddam Marines out of bounds but irrepressible. A couple of dollars here and a couple more there, and along came a rickety Ford truck, about half a mile from camp. Always half a dozen Marines hopped aboard: out of bounds was out of bounds but lust conquered all. They would chat intermittently in the last light, releasing their impatience in brief bursts of small talk. One would polish his boots nervously, boots that he would shortly drag through the dust and rubbish of Hinche's main street, or the rotting garbage that paved Hinche's alleys. 'I used to think the daylight lasted forever in the tropics,' one of them would say, 'but it shuts down about six o'clock like some small town in Georgia.'

'It's a damn funny place and a damn funny war,' another would say. 'Every time we kill one, three or four more jump up.'

'Got to protect the Panama Canal,' one would intone, and the others would cackle; that solemn absurdity issued from Washington.

'Jeez, against who?' was the liturgical response, and the answer to that was always a racial slur, varying only in style and venom: 'Irish. Gone fill it in and plant spuds.' 'Jews. Gone double the tolls.' 'Niggers. Gone sit on the bank and fish.' 'Chinese. Gone line it with washtubs.'

'Gone take a while.'

'Gone take forever. Marine Corp's forever anyway.'

Upon some such gloomy note they would subside for a time. The truck would rattle on, and eventually check with squeals and rattles. 'Tree heure,' the driver would announce. 'Tree heure go beck.'

They hopped from the truck and sought their bearings. The truck clattered away and was replaced by shadowy platoons of children clucking 'fack-fack' like a flock of black chicks. Some cosmopolitan Marine would say, 'Allez, ça va.' An urchin would plead, 'Ba iune gourde, ba iune gourde,' give me one gourde, and what was that now, an American nickel? The children were barefoot, woolly headed, mostly naked, all but featureless in the bleary light of an open-air grog shop, the straining glow of a single oil lamp; their faces were blank and black, their soft voices more music than speech. The Marines strode through them as through stands of black hibiscus. The children trailed, slowed, pleaded.

The men had at first believed that the country women here were worthy but the town women vicious. They also believed that true in their home states. There was agreement among the Marines that hard-working Haitian family women would not be molested. Such women, Gunny Evans pointed out, were rare. McAllister disagreed but held his peace. How could Gunny know the first damn thing about the life of a Haitian woman?

The whorehouses in Hinche were off-limits but not under surveillance, and were mostly daunting hovels. Claps could mean the brig: you could strut down the street high and mighty and go limp on the threshold just thinking about it. The sour smell, too. The inmates were of all shapes, sizes and ages. They were black, bone-poor, swarming, competitive and easy to please. It was rumoured that they trooped out of Hinche's shacks and huts as the jitney trucks appeared on the horizon. Evans summed it up by saying that every goddam woman in Hinche humped and some of them brought their ti moon to watch. That was 'petit monde': children.

So the men dispersed to their favourite hovels. They travelled in pairs. Soon lamps were lit, and men and women laughed in the velvet night.

At open windows the ti moon watched.

McAllister was full of life now, and worried: his heart was not in his work. But he cleaned his weapons, and spent two hours with Flanagan, grooming both his mounts. He tried and failed to keep his mind off Caroline, and on war. 'Men at war, so other men can sit in leather chairs and clip their cigars with gold clippers. I shouldn't be asked to kill, in this mood,' he said.

'You haven't been asked,' Healy said. 'You've been told.'

Next day Dillingham flew out with Wyatt, and McAllister assembled his platoon. He conferred with his new sergeant, an Oklahoman called Neubauer, short and tough, his own age. He caught up on intelligence: Martel's Cacos were chivvying their way in all directions at once, and to the south Batraville's Cacos were fighting Martel as hard as they fought the Marines – right down to drunken brawls in the market. 'The real news comes from our master spy Lafayette,' Healy said. 'He gads about a bit on his day off. Sumbitch knows everything. A real mercenary too. Wants a whole dollar.' He scuffed his camp chair sideways and laid a thick index finger on a hanging map. 'Right here, you see, about a day's ride east, over this range and down into the valley. Several of these small valleys parallel so be careful. There is a village, some forty gentlefolk in normal times, maybe fifty, and about three miles away this farm, a big one, cane and beans and some livestock. It is called La Ferme, which means "the farm".'

'Funny,' McAllister said. 'It also means "shut up".' Healy peered cautiously for veiled ironies, found none, and went on. 'Anyway Lafayette tells me people been drifting in there by twos and threes, and mainly male. They may be joining Martel, or moving in to wait for him, and we will find out what's what. That is, you will. These here *La Vie Parisienne* just arrived, straight from Paris, and I got to catch up on my reading.'

After a briefing and a good sleep they rode out at dawn; the drums seemed to track them all day; and in the evening they bivouacked on a slope above the valley. They set pickets and made a meal and told some lies and smoked, and soon enough dawn came and they were stretching and groaning and trudging off into the bushes, and gargling from canteens and salivating over coffee. Some brushed their teeth and some only gargled. McAllister growled them into formation and they policed the bivouac. The sun rose slowly and late over the hills to the east, and McAllister was uneasy, blinded, his binoculars useless for the moment. He squinted down into the dappled valley. Livestock grazed. Colours were pale and false. Smoke rose from a copse: huts in there. The sky above was pink and pearly.

An hour later he saw more. A stand of cane, a sizeable farmhouse beside a dark blue stream; and upstream, a village in the forest. He lay prone and steadied the glasses on his pack. Tendrils of smoke, a somnolent goat. Cauldrons, or kettles. No human face, no startled figure: a disturbing distant hush. 'Neubauer, you better take a look.'

Neubauer fell beside him and borrowed the

glasses. 'Not a damn soul. But there was ten minutes ago.'

McAllister said, 'Let's go down there and see what's what.'

They reached the farm after a slow prickly ride down the slope, through a peaceful grove of mahogany, and across a stretch of healthy savanna. Only the flash of a yellow bird caught the eye, or a pale lizard, or a busy field rat. The farmhouse was in use, a dwelling, but they – whoever – had seen the blancs coming and were long gone. McAllister noted hearths, iron pots, bowls of grain, beans; the usual scrawny irate chickens. A farm.

'Withdrew across the stream,' Neubauer said. 'Sir.'

'To the village. We'd best move carefully, and have a look.'

They did, and the village was full of life but empty of villagers. Fires burning, stores of food, sheaves of cane, more incurious goats, a houmfort with its altar; but the village was empty.

'They're in the forest,' Neubauer said. 'It is amazing how they can disappear.'

'Look here, sir.'

They joined Clancy in one of the huts. 'Ammo crates,' Neubauer said. 'Stolen thirty-calibre ammunition.'

'Four of 'em,' Clancy said.

'Numbered,' McAllister said. 'We'll take them back.'

Neubauer asked, 'Not going to round up some of these people?'

The village was surrounded by dense forest — cedars, acacias, raintrees, mahoganies. Between the temple and the stream, and curving among the huts like a boulevárd, was a kind of esplanade or pleasance, a village green as at Deux Rochers of cursed memory. Peaceful. Where children would play, does and kids caper. Deux Rochers: they were less than a day's ride from Deux Rochers. But here the silence was eerie. 'No. One ambush a month is enough. We withdraw,' McAllister said. 'I need open country.' All the way out to the treeless fields he felt huge, a target; and even then he wondered who lay hidden in the cane.

They reconnoitreed four villages, all empty. They found no more crates, only a couple of empty sweatstained American cartridge belts. 'It's damn queer,' McAllister said. 'These people are nervous. They've been scared. This is new.'

Neubauer agreed.

'I wish they had an army,' McAllister said. 'Wars are easier to fight when you can see the enemy.'

Neubauer worried. 'You notice even the drums are quiet?'

McAllister had noticed. 'We'll go ask the captain. There must be four or five thousand Cacos within fifty miles of us. Suppose they all gathered together and marched on Hinche?'

Neubauer grinned and patted his rifle. 'It would simplify matters considerably, sir.'

They were five miles east of Hinche, at a place on the plain where many trails converged, when they spotted horsemen. Clancy flung up a hand and they halted. 'That's us,' McAllister said. The setting sun blurred his vision but there was no mistaking horse Marines. 'Half a dozen.'

'They're looking for us,' Neubauer said.

'Clancy! Forward at a trot!'

It was Dillingham with an escort, and McAllister's first thought was peace. On second thoughts he called, 'Is it a general offensive?'

'It's bad news, Mac,' Dillingham replied, and reined in, and his men with him; dust rose.

'Just tell me, Dill. Gunny's dead?'

'I wish that was it,' Dillingham said, and told him.

McAllister was hot-eyed and reckless and dripping sweat. They were standing on the veranda, drinking whiskey now and no one making jokes.

'Her father's been informed,' Healy said. 'He's on his way but it will take time. The colonel has ordered a reduction in patrols and *no* raids. Wyatt has been flying zigzags but hasn't seen a thing.'

'Did they check the gendarmeries? In town, around, all over?'

'Sent word everywhere.'

The camp was in shock. McAllister stood with half a glass of bourbon in one tight hand and saw his men waiting in twos and threes, glancing again and again at the veranda.

Dillingham said, 'If she's been taken somewhere it's for a purpose. They won't hurt her and they'll be in touch.'

'Thanks. Or they'll send pieces of her. Where's Wyatt now?'

'Captain!'

'What is it, Neubauer?'

'You got a nigger lurking.' Neubauer gestured.

The three officers leaned over the side railing. Lafayette hunched and smiled. 'Just keeping himself informed,' Healy said savagely.

Lafayette hopped up and hunched again. 'Mon Capitaine.'

'Shut up and leave us alone,' Healy said.

'La blanche, mon Capitaine.'

'Jesus Christ,' Dillingham said. 'These people. They know everything before it happens.'

'Come up here on the porch,' Healy ordered. They returned to the table and Healy poured more bourbon.

McAllister needed someone to kill. When Lafayette cringed before him, he set a hard hand on the yard-boy's shoulder and said, 'Tell me.'

'Mon Lieutenant.'

'Hurry it up,' Dillingham said.

Lafayette pleaded in silence.

110

'The bastard wants money.'

McAllister slid his hands towards the black throat and said, 'Lafayette, you will tell me right now or I will strangle you. I will strangle you with my bare hands and you will have no last rites and my men will bury you and no one will know or care. Do you understand that?' He said it again, swiftly, in French.

'Oui, mon Lieutenant. Only that in Port-au-Prince they say Martel take la blanche.'

The man was trembling in McAllister's grasp.

'They say.' McAllister grimaced at Healy. 'Your master spy. Our intelligence. Lafayette: what else do they say?'

'No more.'

'What else do they say?'

'I tell you the truth, mon Lieutenant. No more. Please, mon Lieutenant. This is hurt.'

McAllister let him go and sucked down an inch of whiskey. 'Martel was educated by Jesuits. He's not a brute. Captain: when will Wyatt be here?'

'Couple of hours. Coming for you.'

'Yes. I have to go to town.'

'Right. Colonel's cancelled all leave but he wants you there.'

'Hell with the colonel,' McAllister said. 'I want to talk to a priest. I am no goddam use to anybody here and for that matter neither are you two.'

'We have a war to fight.'

'Fuck your war,' McAllister said, surprising himself; the words echoed from another, forgotten, quarrel long ago. He spat off the veranda. He stood at the railing and cursed, long and loud. 'I'll kill them,' he said. Then he hunched like Lafayette and stood struggling with the pain.

Maps. Wyatt tracing his crisscrosses. 'Mainly one or two Haitians beating a loaded donkey. Sometimes a cart. Piccaninnies herding goats. Had one parade over by that Deux Rochers, looked like voodoo, scattered when they saw me. Trouble is I don't know what to look for.'

'She may be in a shack in Port-au-Prince,' McAllister said.

'We'll hear,' Healy said. 'They took her for a purpose and they'll tell us that purpose. Stands to reason.'

'Reason! Wyatt: let's go.'

'What do you want with a priest?' Healy asked.

'To find out where she is,' McAllister said. 'If we go by the book she's dead.'

'We've offered a reward for information,' Colonel Farrell said. 'Every gendarme knows and every agent and double agent and triple agent knows. It's a damn poor country and anybody at all is liable to tell us for money.'

'Including a lot of swindlers who know nothing, sir.'

'We've considered that. We're doing all we can. Colonel Barbour has flown to Southampton and boarded the *Massachusetts;* he'll proceed directly

to Boston and try the rest by plane. I've ordered
defensive patrols only. Washington is firm: we
cannot, ah, offer a replacement. We cannot
exchange an officer for her.'

'Money? Prisoners?'

'We may. It's not ruled out. But nothing can be
done until – '

'Yes. I'd like permission to speak to Haitian
friends, and I'd like an extended leave.'

'You're a serving officer, McAllister.'

'I'm sorry, Colonel, but this war doesn't mean a
damn thing to me now.'

'I regret to hear that.' The colonel straightened,
cold.

'It's an exercise, Colonel. It's like the Philip-
pines and Nicaragua and Cuba and everywhere
they send us – we don't give a damn about these
people. We'll rule the world because there's
nobody else left to rule it, and all we want from
lesser breeds is respect for our law. Well, all I
want from them is my girl.'

'We had best consider all that unsaid,' the
colonel told him. 'Your leave is granted; I'll
inform Healy. If you plan to travel anywhere but
here or Hinche, you will inform me. You will
commit the Corps to nothing, is that understood?'

'Aye aye, sir.'

'Don't lose your nerve, Lieutenant. You didn't
lose your nerve in France.'

* * *

Port-au-Prince was a filthy teeming tropical city full of thieves and traitors. His small open carriage clopped through trash and excrement; exhausted old men lay at the roadside (there was no true gutter); every able-bodied Haitian might be Caco and every door might hide a Caroline, bound and gagged. The stalls, picturesque a week ago, were now merely pathetic: contrived of planks, tin cans, cardboard boxes, offering catchpenny utensils or ageing foodstuffs. And Caroline everywhere and nowhere – he grimaced, told himself to be calm, and unclenched his fists.

The cab halted, the horse drooped, the crowd gathered. McAllister asked, 'On est chez le Père Scarron?'

The cabbie seemed a papery centenarian and was wearing a derby hat. The world was slipping away from McAllister; what was real here? The crowd muttered; a cry, B'jou le blanc! The old man assured him: it was Father Scarron's rectory.

What had McAllister expected? Spires? A porch? A majestic edifice of stone? The rectory was a pleasant, open, two-story tropical house with balconies on the three visible sides of the upper floor. He paid the cabbie and stepped to the door, with its crucifix: he was looking Christ in the eye. McAllister knocked.

In time a young man opened the door, perhaps a novice, a student. 'Father Scarron, please. It's urgent.'

The young man bowed and showed him in.

Thank God, thank God: the priest was at home and not off on a round of rural parishes. The room was spacious, cool, louvreed. A salon, a wall of books. On another wall, a white wall, a map of Hispaniola: Haiti blue, San Domingo green, the sea yellow.

Scarron came forward briskly, but looked sleepless, malarial. They spoke each other's name and shook hands. 'I'm sorry, I'm sick with shame, for all of us. Please sit. You'll take a glass?'

'Thank you.' McAllister set his broad-brimmed campaign hat on an end-table.

Scarron sent the young man for Pommard and two glasses. 'I'm not sure I can tell you more than you know. She has been abducted. She was abducted by four Haitians who are presumed to be Martel's people. There has been no word since. Very likely she is on her way to Martel. A hostage.' He plucked at his soutane, scratched his cheek, glanced at the map.

'You must know more than that. Our yard-boy in Hinche knew that much.'

Scarron made no answer.

The priest was deeply perturbed; McAllister kept at him. 'Martel. Is he a . . . is he a *moral* man, has he any sense of decency at all?'

'He had until the Jesuits got hold of him,' Scarron said. 'Listen to me: he's a serious man, a political leader, a general, and he and his staff can have a thousand women a night without her.'

'You do come to the point. Thanks,' McAllister said. 'How long have you known him?'

'Twenty years, twenty-five.'

'Are you a Caco?'

Scarron said, 'What!'

'I only want to know for tactical reasons. Put it another way: will he listen to you?'

'Saint Rita,' Scarron said. 'The patron saint of the impossible. Now listen. You cannot know what levels of deception we wander through; of irony and condescension and native shrewdness. Let me tell you a story. Three or four years ago when your Major Butler was our dictator, the government was not legal because there were not enough cabinet members. You understand: it was a hazardous occupation. Smedley Butler had a Haitian aide, and asked him to nominate a minister. The aide did so, the government was installed, and Butler congratulated himself: he had cut a Gordian knot, and what did the Haitians know or care about process, law, precedent?'

'It was a start,' McAllister said.

'The new minister's first act was to draw an advance on his salary; his second was to repay a loan of fifty dollars in gold to Butler's aide. Shortly the government died of inanition. Whose was the more delicate sense of irony – Butler's? the aide's? the minister's?'

'You're being polite,' McAllister said. 'You're trying to tell me I can't understand Haiti.'

'I'm trying to tell you that you cannot know what is at stake.'

'But I do know Americans,' McAllister said. 'The Marines have a war to fight and very soon they'll be fighting it as they always do and never mind Caroline, but just now they're shocked, they've paused, and I want to use that pause. I want to go to Martel. I don't give a goddam about irony. I want *you* to go to Martel and do what must be done to bring her home.'

'And then leave Haiti, I suppose.'

McAllister was confused.

'What would become of me? The government would call me Caco; the Cacos would call me a white priest.'

'But it's a woman's life at stake!'

'A white woman's. Your woman's.'

'Yes. But you know her, she's a good woman, it isn't just that I love her, it's that she's *good*, and you're fond of her and why should she pay for my sins? You could go in mufti. Would that help?'

'Never. A priest out of uniform is behind the enemy lines in disguise. I am God's servant, not his spy. Ah, McAllister! Do you know what I am to Martel? Just another blanc. It is not always the skin, you see. When a coal-black Haitian attorney, in a suit from Paris and a cravat and gold pince-nez, comes to my door my houseboy announces, "C'est un blanc, mon père."'

'Is there any other way?' McAllister asked. 'My God, man, think of her out there!'

117

Scarron groaned, and aged before McAllister's eyes: crow's-feet, a downward wrinkle from the corner of the mouth. 'You cannot know what you ask,' the priest said, 'and I cannot refuse you.'

McAllister was again confused. He dismissed the riddles and concentrated on his one discovery: Scarron had not replied, 'Impossible.'

'I can't speak for the Corps,' McAllister said, 'but I'll fight like hell for whatever we need. An aircraft, gold, a truce, he can have me.'

'He won't bargain,' Scarron said. 'He's a large man in all ways. He has no idea who his parents were but he is a man of breeding.'

'Yes. A well-bred gentleman who kidnaps young women. I'm sick of him. I'm tired of hearing he's God.'

'He's not my God,' Scarron said wearily, touching the black crucifix that lay against his white soutane. 'My God is the God of Abraham, Isaac, Jacob, Michelangelo and Bach: all I want is the white past and a black future. But Haitians worship many gods, and Martel is one of them. He has known obscurity and resisted temptation and preached from the mountaintop. Now he is scourging the moneychangers and promising Haiti eternal life.'

The houseboy served wine, and the men sipped in silence.

After a time Father Scarron said, 'We are an immensely proud people, and for over a century we have done nothing whatever to be proud of.'

6

Caroline Barbour had fallen asleep in a four-poster, safe within a cocoon of mosquito netting furnished by the Marine Corps; and she was born again in a shroud, in a wagon, in a tropical forest. In a stupor too: this was an unusually vivid nightmare, her limbs heavy, immobile, no escape. Aches and pains – her elbows, her hips, the back of her head – roused her further, and were replaced by nausea and then fear – a bolt of pure painful terror, like a thunderclap that stops the breath and freezes the heart.

She fumbled and groped: she was swathed in perhaps a sheet, and she was clothed in her own proper nightgown, and the soft parts of her body were warm and comfortable. She smelled horse; she tasted medicine. 'I should scream,' she said aloud. But of course it was a dream, it must be: the sharp suffocating fear, and soon the surge of relief that left one limp. Yet she lay on a pallet that crackled softly, and she breathed in odours of the stable, and heard a musical Creole voice – and the cart creaked and groaned, and a beast staled, with a hissing spatter.

She was journeying through the night in a wagon. A grey sky, black boughs above: perhaps dawn, or a clouded moon.

She was too sleepy to scream. Yes. Too weary to understand. It would be all right. Something to do with Bobby. She was a princess clothed in cobwebs.

In memory she saw a vaulted ward, and ranks of beds, but she was not in Paris; she was immensely tired. She was also terribly afraid, but of what? No, this was not Paris, but the familiar odour, the ward – alcohol? ether? Haiti, yes, she was in Haiti, a tropical night, and dreaming. She shifted, and the pain died; she snuggled into the straw. 'I am too tired to discuss it now,' she said aloud, and she dropped into the void.

She floated in light, squinted, and fear possessed her: she lay ice-cold in the tropical morning. 'My God,' she cried, and struggled to sit; a headache stunned her like a blow. The green forest, a wagon creaking and groaning, a mule in the traces, two black men trudging before. One reached for the bridle, and the wagon halted; they contemplated Caroline. Behind her a voice said, 'Allez, va,' and the two men returned to their trudging, one tugging briefly at the bridle.

Now her fear was like fire; she waited, breathing deeply; it burned itself out. The headache was murderous. 'I am a colonel's daughter,' she said, and again in French.

Behind her a voice said, 'Good morning.' She turned, and was dizzy.

A man on horseback tipped his sombrero politely, a white man.

Caroline was not prepared for this apparition, so she inspected him in silence. He was clean-shaven but for a generous moustache, and tanned or naturally swarthy. His features were bold, the thick black brows striking and the eyes a cold blue; he seemed to be focusing on a point at the centre of her forehead. He sat a horse well, and it was a fine horse he sat. Caroline said, 'Good morning. Who are you?'

He might have frowned.

Caroline was quiet for a time: she wiped her eyes on the hem of her nightgown, and rubbed her teeth with a finger. Nature was kind, she realized: the truth was seeping slowly through her headache, and as she grew less numb – a drug, yes, a drug wearing off – she had time to rally. She remembered soldiers confiding, 'At first, you see, I was in shock, so when they told me I had lost my legs I almost shrugged. Oh yes, lost my legs. Oh yes, it's raining. Oh yes, soup for supper. Then when I hated them for it and wanted to die, it was too late: I was stronger and wanted to live.' By the time she thought of rape she was Caroline again, groggy, doubtless dull of eye, nursing a terrible headache and a worse fear, but Caroline Barbour the famous colonel's daughter.

'I need to drink,' she said. 'I need to wash.'

Their little caravan was pacing a trodden path, not much used but not overgrown. 'There was a yellow butterfly,' a soldier had told her, 'and as I could not move my limbs I resigned from the army and studied this butterfly.' Beside the trail grew oleander, and sometimes a tall red bush, virtually a tree, of bougainvillaea. Turtle-doves shot across their path, or rose in a flutter as the men and the mule approached. The sun had risen but was screened by the forest; the day was bright but still cool.

If they had meant to do her harm, they would have done it by now.

She believed that. She was still sleepy, and her head throbbed angrily, and the green morning was warm; she lay back, and hugged herself. She would not weep whatever happened.

Shortly she wept, and then drifted off.

Later she heard the swirl and gurgle of a flowing stream, and they turned off the trail, halting at a cluster of huts festooned with vines and blossoms. One of the Haitians called, 'Ohé, la femme!' Already villagers had loomed in doorways. Naked children goggled or hid their faces. A stout woman emerged from one hut, folded her arms, and considered these signs and portents. She dismissed the Haitians and animals, concentrating on the two blancs. She wore a dark blue cotton tunic, and her breasts were huge.

'B'jou, maman,' said the rider, and dismounted. Creole flew past Caroline like a flock of doves; she grasped it on the wing, and understood a bit. 'This woman must start the day, maman, even as you and I. Take her to the water, will you, and bring her back? We could use a meal, too. The sun is long up.'

'Slowly, slowly,' the woman said. Men emerged too, and gaped; other women, many children. A cock crowed. Caroline heard no drums; even in Port-au-Prince distant drums had pulsed; but this morning was cool and pleasant and silent, the hush so perfect that a drop of water falling on a stiff leaf echoed like a gunshot. The village stood in a long glade, and among the huts chickens pecked and jerked. The huts wore roughly conical roofs, and smoke hovered.

The stout woman advanced to the cart for a closer view of Caroline; she reached out to touch the pale cheek, and clucked.

Caroline slurred French: 'Yes. Please take me to the stream.'

The woman said, 'Eh! Who is this now? Was she talking about the stream?'

One of the muleteers said, 'You heard, maman. She speaks white French.'

'I understood, I understood. And who are you all and why should we give you food?'

The white man said, 'We'll pay. If one could get on with it, and talk later?'

'Ah, pay.'

'That's better,' a male villager said with stern dignity.

'Shut up,' the woman said. She smiled at Caroline, stretched forth a plump black hand and said, 'Come with me now.'

Caroline rose carefully; her head no longer ached and none of her limbs was asleep, but she was dismayingly aware of her nightgown, purchased chez Worth, scooped low and ruffled at the neck, and cut daringly high at the hem, with an echo of the ruffle not more than four inches below the knee. Useful antidotes to fear: hunger and modesty. She clutched the gown properly to her, but disembarking from a wagon demanded exercise, even acrobatics, and she was lightheaded.

For the first time, Caroline set a bare foot on Haitian soil. The ground was damp: a recent shower.

She shot a dark glance at the sombrero'd man: he was expressionless, emotionless, his eyes like blue crystal: he might have been blind. Again dread plucked at her, twanged. She descended, and took refuge with the stout, very black Haitian woman.

The woman's hair was short and woolly, her face fat and round, her small black eyes unreadable.

'Please,' Caroline whispered, 'take me to the water,' and then she found herself, colonel's daughter or no, fighting tears, and tugging at her nightgown to wipe her running nose on a ruffle. She flinched when the woman raised a hand.

'Hey, hey, no one will hurt you,' said the Haitian woman. 'Come with me now.' And she stretched forth a plump black hand, the palm pink.

Caroline clasped the hand, and followed.

They walked downstream along the bank, and at some way from the village the woman tapped herself, saying 'Yolette,' and struggled out of her tunic, standing bulky and naked while she hung it from a branch.

Caroline said, 'Yolette.'

The woman said, 'Vee-olette. Yolette, moins. Ou? Z'appeller?'

'Caroline.'

Yolette was pleased. 'Caroline.' She then ignored the blanche. She stepped into the stream, stirred up the water to no obvious purpose, and squatted. Caroline did not understand, and then she did understand.

She had been hearing little peeps, like chicks: these were tree frogs. A lizard scurried at her feet. Yolette walked upstream, to her thighs in the rush and gurgle; she turned and beckoned. A woman: breasts, haunches, the dense black brush between her legs, the roll of her heavy buttocks. Caroline found motion if not will: she peered about, saw no one else, in a dream drew the nightgown over her head, hung it from another branch, and hastened to the stream.

Other women joined them, first peeking shyly through the shrubs, then advancing naked and stately to enter the water. Little girls too, who were fascinated by her white skin. Perhaps they had never seen a white woman before. Surely not a white woman naked. This audience flustered Caroline; her hands covered her floating breasts, and she peered again into the forest for lurking men. The stream swirled and splashed; she rubbed herself with gritty sand from the bed, took a full breath, ducked her head, scrubbed her face with both hands and cleaned her teeth with a finger until one of the women handed her a split twig and demonstrated. Some of these women were flat-chested; it seemed a contradiction; but why, after all? Perhaps she was full of odd notions. They all carried little leather bags on thongs about the neck. She wondered what gods they worshipped.

Yolette was evidently struck by the absence of hair in Caroline's armpits. Caroline made snipping motions with two fingers and said, 'Couper, pour . . .' but stopped right there. Pour . . . quoi? The manners and morals of modern youth: French, piano, watercolours, and couper pour . . . The women were laughing. Couper! Caroline too laughed, but the laughter caught in her throat and vanished in the horrible taste of dread. What was she being prepared for?

But among the women, in the early sunlight, the water clean and cool and her body too, she believed she might survive. When she flowed naked on to the bank, she even felt beautiful.

But once on the bank she was embarrassed and

angry; she took refuge amid the women, dried herself on her ruffles and grew calmer when the girls giggled: they seemed obsessed by her white breasts and pink nipples. She slipped into the nightgown. Yolette, no longer a stranger, patted her own grand belly with groans of sad deprecation, like any matron gone to flesh. Caroline sympathized: 'I am young and lucky.'

'So you are,' said Yolette, 'as I was once. Time passes and the men make pigs of us, with their clairin and their bamboo. But that is life.'

Caroline wondered what bamboo had to do with this, but only asked, 'Have you many children?'

'Nine,' said Yolette. 'Six of them dead.'

In a clearing among the huts a cooking fire smoked. Caroline was permitted to eat a fried plantain from a wooden plate with her fingers: it was manna. She took her turn at a stone jug, and spluttered and choked as it seared her belly. Women tittered, men crowed: 'A litte tot of rum to start the day,' Yolette said.

The men of the village were fascinated; they cocked their heads, murmured, laughed easily. Caroline's captors stood apart and did not laugh. She wanted to ask the blanc why she was here, but his eyes were empty and roamed beyond her. The two Haitians wore long knives; the blanc a pistol and a knife. She remembered a rifle in a scabbard at his saddle. Afoot he seemed smaller and less powerful. Bobby was taller and stronger. Bobby would hear; Bobby would come.

She asked Yolette: 'Why have they brought me here?'

Yolette was amazed. 'The blanc is not your man?'

Once the blanc looked directly at her, and she turned away, chilled to the heart. The two Haitians inspected her and made little jokes. The blanc contemplated them as if he planned to make them vanish: they subsided and seemed to shrink. One was too tall and the other too short. The taller wore dirty white cotton trousers and a white dress shirt with no collar and buttoned cuffs, as if he feared the sun; and he wore a gold ring, set with a sparkling gem; but he wore no hat. The shorter wore blue cotton trousers, no shirt, only the little leather bag like a pendant, and a grimy tan felt hat with the brim down. She saw now that their knives were not knives but machetes.

When the time came to leave, Caroline despaired; a sob gathered, and she fought it back. She stood before the blanc and said, 'Who are you?'

'What difference should that make?'

'Then *what* are you?'

'Ah,' he said, and after a moment, 'just a soldier.'

The taller Haitian stroked her cheek, considered the texture of her, said, 'Ha,' and stepped away. The blanc spoke one word. The tall Haitian spat.

He sniggered, muttered to the little one, and walked a few steps so that he could swagger.

They were hotter now in the risen sun, and the day's aromas were rich: human sweat, the mule, woodsmoke, dung.

'I want men's clothes,' she said.

After a time the blanc shrugged. 'Maman!' Yolette came to them, and he explained; Yolette approved, and bustled away. On one of the doorposts Caroline saw a crucifix: a fat metallic snake was twined about a wooden cross. The clothes were found: long blue trousers and a blue slipover shirt with loose sleeves to the elbow. They were clean; they smelled fresh. Caroline stepped behind the wagon and changed quickly. Only the blanc was shod, in low boots; Caroline did not ask for footwear. Should she offer the nightgown to maman? No.

When he saw her dressed the blanc said, 'Good. We may have to leave the cart, and put you on the mule. Can you ride?'

'Oh yes, I can ride,' Caroline said, 'astride; and I can take a five-foot jump.'

'It will be a rare sight,' he said. 'The mule can't.'

She looked for the man behind the flat, blind, blue eyes, but found no one.

Time moves slower through a thick cold medium like fear; by nightfall Caroline had been a month on the trail. The blanc never spoke; the Haitians glanced hungrily or with contempt – why? – at their huddled captive. They passed villages, and children lined the path in naked ranks, wide-eyed and silent, then giggling and joking. Their elders joined them. The cart groaned along: Caroline said 'B'jou' to the Haitians and scattered answers comforted her. The villagers were of many shades, and she recalled Father Scarron: one hundred and twenty-eight, he had joked. She prayed aloud, as if in conversation: 'Ah God: help me. Tell me where I am and why.' She begged the blanc: 'Will you please tell me why?'

He made no answer, only rode along behind her like a zombie: no smile and no frown, no chat, never spat or blew his nose. He rode down a narrow side trail once. She waited in rising fear, and he returned in two or three minutes.

Another village, more Haitians. Long headed, round headed, great flashing mouthfuls of teeth and also toothless elders. Some noses round and some sharp, and in one clearing a moustachioed man with his trousers stuffed into boots, a Spanish look about him, a horseman. She could not be more than twenty or twenty-five miles from Port-au-Prince with its ministries and markets and docks; she might have been in the heart of Africa, or South America. Once they heard the buzz of an aircraft, like the whining drone of an angry dragonfly; the blanc spoke, the wagon trundled off the trail, and they paused in welcome shade until the hum faded and vanished.

Caroline was allowed some minutes' privacy in

the evening, and when she woke beneath the stars and peered over the side of the cart, the blanc nodded briefly, sitting with his back to a tree, his sombrero on the ground beside him. She asked quietly, 'You never sleep?'

And again he made no answer.

The villages were not all alike. She saw clusters of shacks in lowland clearings, near fields of scraggly parched greens. She saw huts all but hidden in rain forest and foliage. Again at sunrise she was permitted to join the women – in the same stream? another? A woman shouted towards the bank, and several made angry faces; bushes trembled, and the women scoffed. A watcher: this outlandish white animal: what man would not peep? Would Bobby peep? Perhaps, and then turn away ashamed, a solemn lusty gentleman and hypocrite. Oh God, Bobby! She contracted in pain.

Caroline ate plantain, beans, sweet gourd, dried goat. She drank fresh water and fresh rum, and hid her grief – fears, rising tears. Later that morning she and her captors halted before a grave. It was marked by a great flat rock, as if to forestall any sudden resurrection, and there were two crosses: one painted white on the rock and one of wood planted in the earth. On the rock were small wooden plates of rice and greens, with small yellow-and-black birds fluttering among them; and a cup, empty. A tumbled flowery vine embellished the grave. 'Petraea,' she murmured.

'Liane Saint-Jean, they call it.' It was the blanc; she gasped.

'How odd,' she managed. 'Peter becomes John. Why the food and drink?'

'For the dead,' he said. 'In time it is all eaten, so they set out more.'

'Please,' she said. 'What do you want with me?'

A hummingbird hovered and darted. Sunlight snaked through branches and dappled the grave.

That day the two Haitians pricked out their clothing and hair with bits of red cloth and thread. So they were Cacos. And the blanc? Were there white Cacos?

She asked him. 'Are you a Caco?'

'Oh yes,' he said. His voice was American, not British; northern; she remembered hard *r*'s.

They were travelling just below a ridge, so the sun set too soon but the light lingered. The evening cooled quickly and the men cheered up; the Haitians shared a canteen, and fumes of clairin wafted back to Caroline. The canteen cover was olive drab. By now she was facing the Caco blanc and travelling backwards, talking at him over the tailgate. 'It's inhuman not to tell me.' She wondered: he might be silent not merely by custom or malevolence but because the game amused him. So she played. 'Are you afraid I'll kill myself? How? What do you suppose they're saying in Port-au-Prince?' He had uttered few words, but each was a plus: when he did speak she was a woman and not a piece of merchandise. Baggage. Bobby had called her a scheming baggage, and had kissed her soundly.

The cart creaked to a halt, and she heard a whistle. She turned: the larger Haitian was grinning. The blanc's voice rapped out, nothing she could decipher. The Haitian's grin died, and he showed a sullen countenance; his companion glanced from him to the blanc, and spoke urgently. The larger Haitian patted his own private parts and offered Caroline an obvious invitation. She understood the blanc to say, 'That's enough,' but the Haitian went on, crooning, while she gazed, fearful and fascinated; and abruptly he fell silent, and his hand went to the hilt of his machete. The other Haitian went on glancing, nervous and excited.

Caroline turned to the blanc. His expression had not altered, and he spoke again, the voice low and almost ingratiating, and she was sure she understood: 'Try it. Killing is my trade.'

The Haitian turned away, and muttered to his smaller companion.

'I'll need sleep,' the blanc said. 'Can you fire a revolver?'

'Yes.'

'You won't play games. I'm your bodyguard, and I'm not sure these two are even on my side.'

'No.'

'It's just to keep watch while I sleep for a few hours.'

'Yes. Why have you done this?'

But he had no more to say.

That night they built a fire, and ate hot food and drank hot coffee. 'I'll sleep in the cart with you,' he said.

'No.'

'I'm too tired,' he said, 'and it will keep the others away. While I sleep, you watch. Understand? I can go two nights but not three.'

'These men drink.'

'So do I, now and then,' he said. 'They're men and may molest you; wake me if there's time. If not, shoot them dead. Could you do that?'

'Yes.' They were all four seated about the fire chatting, and she had just announced that she could kill two of them.

'You seem sure,' he said. 'Have you killed before?'

'Rabbits and birds. With a shotgun.'

'Did you dress them?'

'Yes, and ate them.'

In the firelight he showed white teeth. 'It's a start.'

'What shall I call you?'

He pondered this. 'Sergeant,' he said.

'Were you a Marine? A soldier?'

But he had exhausted his small talk.

There was no moon, but starshine gleamed off broad leaves. For long minutes the silence was perfect, and then life stirred in the forest: perhaps only the breeze, a rustle, a snap. The mule drooped, and broke wind frequently. The sergeant slept on his back, now and then emitting a gentle snore; his rifle lay beside him, his right hand loose upon it.

Caroline shifted. She prayed, with no real conviction. The revolver was warm in her hand, and her palm grew moist; she set the pistol beside her. The whole Corps would be searching for her. Her father would be on his way to Port-au-Prince. Bobby would be plunging through the forest at the head of a battalion.

No. Who knew where she was? Well, the villagers, and she knew how Haitians gossiped.

Why had they done this?

Ransom. To buy arms and ammunition. Or to force a truce?

Truce. Her father in Paris. Bobby in Paris, Bobby's embrace . . . Bobby's wounds . . .

She woke at the creak of a board; she was still in Paris. She heard a man whisper, 'Ssssh,' and smelled the fumes of rum. An animal blew, the breeze sighed, beside her a man snored raucously.

She poked viciously at the blanc, groped for the revolver, found it; her right hand closed on it as she saw a figure loom over the far side of the wagon – of course, they would kill the sergeant first, oh God, no panic, two hands, steady – then a confusion of bulk and the wagon rocking, a mass swaying in the starlight. She fired. The roar was shattering, and then it was all too quick, a thud, a scramble, silence. She was sitting rigid, the revolver in both hands. 'Speak,' she gasped. 'Who is it? Qui moon?'

'It's me,' the sergeant said, climbing back aboard. 'You damn near killed me.'

'I'm sorry,' she whispered. She gasped. 'Where is he? Who was it?'

'The big Caco.' The blanc seemed to gasp also, and she heard a hoarse 'Khhhaaa!'

'Are you hurt?'

He strangled, and exploded; he coughed for a full minute. He wiped his mouth with straw, pulled out a bandanna and wiped it again. He dabbed at his shirt and trousers. 'Christ. He bled all over me.'

'Cold water,' she whispered. 'Cold water will wash away blood. What . . . Who bled?'

'The Caco.'

'Where is he?'

'On the ground. Dead. Go back to sleep.'

Carefully Caroline set down the pistol and knelt, her back to him; carefully she vomited over the side of the wagon. She too wiped her mouth with a handful of straw, and then on the hem of her shirt. 'How could he bleed so much?'

'I had my knife in him when you fired. This is real trouble, lady.'

'Imagine.'

'I don't mind killing,' he said. 'Most men don't. Ask your daddy some time.'

'But you don't like this.'

136

'No, I sure do not. In this country, you never know who you're killing. Ten years later some cousin poisons your coffee. I don't know who he was but he mattered.'

'How do you know that?'

'By the way he answered me back. And I believe this is a real diamond in his ring; we'll see in daylight. He acted like an only child that they spoiled rotten.'

'I'm an only child.'

'That's what I mean,' he said. 'Spoiled. All you had to do was stay awake.'

'Where's the little one?'

'Ran like a rabbit. You fell asleep.'

'I'm sorry, I'm sorry. God help me.'

'God help us both now. If the little fellow comes back with ten or twenty more we're in trouble. Listen to me. I'm taking you to a man called Martel, and once we reach him we're safe – '

'Safe!'

' – but there's about five thousand other fellows out there would like to deliver the merchandise and bank the profits. I'm your best bet and don't fool with me.'

She died again.

He glanced at the stars: 'You gave me about two hours' sleep. Maybe in the morning I sleep some more. First one?' In the faint glow he was grinning like a jackal.

'First what?'

'You killed him.'

137

It was at last too much: it was happening to someone else: no, it was not: it had not happened at all: yes, it had. 'Leave me alone,' she moaned, and shuddered, with a long racking sob. She saw his dim hand take up the pistol, heard him vault from the wagon; she lay prone and despaired. Would it be better to die now?

No. Not ever.

'For Christ's sake,' he said. 'Now *I'm* bleeding.'

She sat up, steadied herself with a deep breath. 'Where? How badly?'

'My left arm. Bastard sliced me with his machete.'

'Does it hurt?'

'Yes, it hurts. I don't care about that. But I need the blood. Help me – no, forget it.'

'Keep quiet,' she said. 'Sit still. Take off your shirt. Give me your bandanna and canteen.'

'Canteen's on my saddle,' he said.

She clambered off the wagon. One foot came down on a warm body and she flinched, but she had crossed a frontier and there was no recrossing, no return ever. Perhaps blood now stained her foot: no matter. The horse, hitched to the tailgate, whuffled low and shied. She spoke to him, stroked his muzzle, blew warm breath into his nostrils. He stood gentle. She found the canteen and unhooked it, and returned to the wagon, padding carefully.

The sergeant's shirt was off. She saw the cut, the blood oozing and not running. Hanging about

138

his neck was a small bag on a rawhide thong. 'You'll be fine,' she said. 'That's a ouanga bag, isn't it?'

'Shut up,' he said.

She washed the wound. 'Needs stitches.'

'Tie it up.'

'You'll have a scar.'

At that he convulsed again, and she paused, awaiting the cough. But he was laughing, a startling joyless sound.

She proceeded with her work. 'If it soaks through too fast we'll need a tourniquet. Have you another bandanna?'

'Belt,' he said. 'Your cuff. Braided grass. Lariat. Where'd you learn this?'

'Paris.'

He was silent again; she saw his face close. Then he asked, 'Hospital? The war? Colonel's daughter does her bit?'

'Yes,' she said. 'You'll do. Sleep a while. Or will he come back?'

'Not tonight. Will you stay awake anyway?'

'I will.'

He replaced the spent cartridge, his left arm moving stiffly, and he handed her the pistol. 'You're crying.'

'Of course I'm crying. This is a nightmare.'

An insomniac dove cooed insistently, and an errant breeze soothed them. She looked desperately for the man within, as if his soul might shine out. In the obscurity his gaze was steady and without passion. After two or three minutes he raised his sound arm and stroked her hair. Slowly he brought her face to his; he kissed her roughly. He drew away, eased the pistol from her hand, set it between them, and kissed her again.

He tasted of blood.

She was still quite shaky, but took up the pistol, and with the muzzle jabbed him in the ribs.

'You need a man,' he said.

'I just killed a man,' she said. 'Besides, we haven't been introduced.'

7

Saint Rita's: built of stone and wood, 1809; razed
and raised a dozen times; built of stone and wood,
1909, and stained glass, mahogany pews, marble
font, a spacious vestibule, in the transept four
confessional boxes. Nothing of the cathedral: it
was too squat, too sunny: only the gold of stained
glass and a touch of West Indian baroque on the
porch, black archangels, 'my piccaninny putti'.
Within, a high altar, from which Father Scarron
gazed out, at Christmas and Easter, over three
hundred worshippers, some of them known athe-
ists who venerated Voltaire, others rumoured par-
ticipants in vodun who venerated Damballa and
Papa Legba; a few were both, or all three – and
why not? The three in one; or the ancient panthe-
ons; or sermons in stones and good in every thing.
Their ancestors had worshipped fire and thunder,
rain and tree, lions and leopards; had coupled in
the fields to make the land fertile; and had been
captured, exiled, auctioned by Christians.

He knelt, alone in his own church; it was cool
and dark like a grotto. He rummaged his soul for a
supreme emotion, and found the void. 'Oh Christ,'
he said in English.

'There were four of us,' the man had confessed:
a soft troubled tenor.

'Go on, my son.'

'We took the blanche for Martel. I knew it was wrong and I tried not to help. And now I am sick.'

Father Scarron too was sick: 'And the other three?'

'I must not. Only . . .'

'Only?'

'Only one was a son of Fleury. On the left hand but a son.'

Fleury: therefore Martel. Patron and protector, as who should say, godfather. 'And where is the blanche now?'

'On her way. I only helped carry her to a cart. They spoke of a blanc.'

'A blanc. A Marine?'

'The white Caco, they said.' He knew nothing more about this soldier. He was a fearful sinner and ignorant. He did not know who had ordered the abduction. Perhaps Fleury. Fleury ruled the north. One did not say no to Fleury.

When the man fell quiet Father Scarron said, 'This is a terrible thing you have done.' Then he could not speak at all for some moments. For her, Hell is Haiti now. And a terrible thing you have done to me too; could you not have found another confessor? Scarron asked for details like an official and not a priest; and in the end he gave the man penance and absolution like a priest and not an official.

Alone, struggling to pray, he leaned forward, pressed his forehead hard against the pew, sought pain. 'Help me, Christ,' he managed. 'Help me, my friend Jesus. No bishop and no pope can help me, only you.'

Father Scarron trudged through the Haitian night. Life surged calmly along the streets and roads; deeper in the alleyways angry cries and short laughter told him of lives less calm. What could a priest know of wife-beating or empty bellies? Father, I have fornicated — scarcely worth reporting. I doubt. I harbour impure thoughts. I covet, steal, blaspheme. Never did they say, Father, I am hungry. Hunger is a sin. Father, my child is going blind. Blindness is a sin. Father, I can neither read nor write; I am an ignorant animal, and that is a sin.

And if they did come to him with those woes, what would he tell them?

He entered the gaguerre unremarked, proceeded to the bar, and fortified himself with one clairin, immediately ordering a second. The night was ordinary — full of sound and colour, handlers debating and bettors shouting; rather more whores than usual. He was wearing work-men's clothes and a battered broad-brimmed straw hat, and cowhide sandals. He contemplated the cocks with no real interest, and from time to time glanced down at his sandals, or adjusted his hat. A priest out of uniform. Behind the enemy lines in disguise. These? His enemy?

He made his way slowly to Boniface's loge.

Outside the door he sat upon the ground, leaned back against the palisade, tipped his hat forward and sipped in privacy.

Boniface was not long. Scarron heard him ask, 'And who is this?', and the priest removed the straw hat and offered a reluctant smile.

Boniface said, 'Good God, Father.'

Boniface was nonplussed: a rare moment. Another night this might have amused Scarron, but now, and perhaps forevermore, the priest was heavy laden. 'Hey, Bobo,' he said. 'How goes it?'

'Fine and dandy — but what are you doing in that costume?' He sighed, ah, ah: 'So you know. You know . . . something.'

'Yes.'

In the flickering torchlight Boniface was solid, a monument, enviable and certain: whatever befell Haiti, Boniface would endure. 'On your feet,' he said. 'Nothing is that bad. Into the loge. Dump that horse-piss; I have some Jamaican.'

They sat upon the floor. Father Scarron found the isolation, the closed door, rather soothing. God was not mocked, of course, God was not excluded, but the privacy was a comfort.

'How did you hear?'

Scarron only shook his head. Boniface, he knew, was never one to rush a quarrel. They drank companionably for a time. Boniface offered tobacco; Scarron declined with thanks. They listened to the crowd.

'I am not one of you,' Scarron said. 'You know that.'

'We never counted on you.'

'Whose rotten idea was it?' He had not expected an answer, and after a pause he went on: 'Barbarous. In the name of liberty. You call yourself an idealist, I suppose.'

'I call myself a Haitian. What do you call yourself?'

'You must tell me where she is,' Father Scarron said. 'Or at least where he is.'

'Someone else will tell you; not I.'

'I must see him,' Scarron said. 'You must tell me.'

Boniface shrugged. 'There is no "must" for me. The "must" is for you: you must choose.'

'Between what and what?'

'Between your own people and the others.'

'First I must decide which is which,' Father Scarron said. 'Will you help me? How long have we been friends?'

'We've been friends for ten years and no I will not help you.' And more roughly, 'You're one of *them*, you know. This whole conversation is silly.'

'Boniface!' The priest's tone was passionate, harsh. 'This is a foolish young woman who is no part of Haiti's quarrels.'

'And is a blanche,' Boniface said. 'Would you be here if it were some scrawny black whore from an alleyway?'

Scarron bowed his head.

'How long have you been a priest?' Boniface asked.

'Twelve years.'

'And how long have you been black? And you will really do this, for a blanche?'

'No. As usual, for something larger and indefinable. A last favour?'

Boniface sat impassive.

'Who is the white Caco? Is he really white?'

Boniface shrugged, and shook his head. 'God help you. You're a good man in your way but it is the wrong way. Go to Hinche and start there. Some advice?'

'Please.'

'Wear your vestments always.'

The disguise had been melodrama, a mortification by wardrobe. In the morning he dressed properly, but for the broad straw hat, and sought McAllister, first at the hotel; then at Olofsson's, which the Marines had converted to home, infirmary, tavern; and then at the Caserne Barracks, a name he detested: 'caserne' meant 'barracks' and what kind of ignoramus ruled Haiti now? And how could such quibbles even enter his mind? He addressed the duty officer in Creole, then in French.

Another officer, a little fellow, said, 'Jesus Christ. He wants McAllister.' This officer wore wings above his breast pocket. 'Tell him McAllister is a Protestant. Ask him if he speaks English.'

'You had better let me see someone,' Father Scarron said. 'It is about Caroline Barbour.'

The pilot sat surly, but the duty officer rose immediately. 'Follow me, Father.'

'Yes, of course, a standing order,' Colonel Farrell said. 'Any news whatever from any source whatever. Please be seated. Let me send word to McAllister.'

Again books and maps; and what could the priest learn from them today? Gibbon, of all antichrists! But a darling funny man. And these military histories; a French dictionary; histories of Haiti too, and a couple in French! One could like these people. Still, they will blame this on all of us.

The colonel returned. 'He'll be along. Can you tell me? You look . . . perturbed.'

'Red-eyed and sore, wrestling with my God.'

Courteously the colonel waited.

'She was taken by four men. She is on her way to Martel. Two of the men were unknown to my . . . informant. The other was – I am sorry to have to tell you this – I am sorry to tell you this – I am sorry – I am sorry – '

Still the colonel waited.

The priest slumped. 'He was a son of Fleury.'

'Fleury.' The colonel reflected. 'Martel's master.'

'His backer; his patron. Martel accepts no master.'

'And where is Martel?'

'I have reason to believe that he is not far from Hinche. More than that I cannot tell you.'

'Because you know nothing more? Or . . . divided loyalties?'

'Divided loyalties,' Father Scarron said, 'but I do not think that you and I mean the same by that.'

The colonel mulled this. 'Well, never mind for now. We'd already heard it was Martel, you know. We don't even need spies; gossips volunteer. We've assembled what we have on Martel's whereabouts – Batraville's too, Savoie's too. And Fleury's son is not Fleury. Appraise Martel for me – what sort of man is he?'

'Larger than life,' Scarron said. 'Strong, cunning. May I say a patriot?'

'Yes. The last refuge of a scoundrel?'

'He is no scoundrel,' Scarron said.

'Miss Barbour has probably not reached his camp. There's a chance we can talk to him first. You'll help us?'

'Anything,' Scarron said.

'Would Fleury help?'

'Never. He hates the blancs perfectly. His hatred is a work of art.'

'Who was the fourth man?'

'I fear I can say nothing of him.'

'Is he here in Port-au-Prince?'

'Nothing whatever.'

'Ah. The confessional. I understand.'

'Do you then? I do not. When a crime is to be committed against the pouvoir établi, I may speak. But when all the authority is established by white invaders . . .'

The colonel was sympathetic. 'Shall we say "allies"? But I understand.'

Father Scarron did not contradict him, but he wondered if anyone not a priest could really understand. And where was McAllister?

They stood by the car, outside the barracks. Wyatt was already fuming beside the driver. McAllister's duffel bag lay on the back seat.

'I'll tell it all to Captain Healy,' McAllister said. 'He's a waggish man but a disciplined officer.' McAllister was a large and healthy fellow, and today he seemed a blind grey hulk.

'I understand disipline,' Scarron said.

'He's from Alabama.'

Scarron shrugged.

'So am I,' Wyatt grumbled.

'Have you flown before?'

'Never,' said the priest.

'It's dangerous,' Wyatt said. 'People vomit.'

McAllister said, 'Shut up, Wyatt.'

Wyatt subsided.

'It's noon now. The corporal will pick you up here about a quarter to two. We'll expect you in Hinche by about four. You can lunch here in the mess, if you'd like.'

Wyatt snorted.

'The colonel has invited me,' Scarron said. 'A discussion of policy. He will tell me what the Marine Corps can and cannot do, and what I may and may not do in their name.'

McAllister made a sour face. 'Yes. Rules. We've had cables from Washington, cables from Colonel Barbour. Do's and don'ts. By the book. But there is no book for this. Never mind what they say. You've got to take me to Martel.'

'The book. You remind me: I must fetch a breviary.'

'Whatever you need,' McAllister said. 'We'll go along now. Thank you, Father. I thank you from the heart.' The two shook hands. McAllister climbed into the car and slammed the door; the car shuddered and rattled, and they sped away.

The colonel added little to what Scarron knew. The colonel admired independence, liked Haiti, respected its intellectuals. The problem of self-government was knotty. The United States, for example, was eighty-five years old in 1861, presumably a mature republic, and the bloodiest war in its history was its Civil War. At what point was the United States ready for self-government?

The colonel seemed pleased with his even-handed view of history. Scarron was astonished that the man could even consider such matters. The priest picked at his ham and yam, sipped without enthusiasm at a white wine. Time lagged; the sun stood still.

'You'll be safe?' the colonel asked. 'You're sure?'

'One is never sure. But in the hills they long for a priest. You cannot detach McAllister?'

'None. Policy. Transcends individuals.'

'Which rather leaves it up to me.'

'We're most grateful,' the colonel said. 'My government, the whole Corps. I hope we can find a way to thank you properly.'

'Miss Barbour alive and well will be my thanks.'

'Amen to that.'

'In there,' Wyatt said. 'In the back.'

Father Scarron clambered aboard, stowed his little black bag between his feet and set his hat upon it.

Wyatt was standing beside the aircraft, with a helmet and goggles extended on one flat hand. Scarron waited. Wyatt's face was a battleground.

Scarron asked, 'Are you Catholic?'

Wyatt said, 'No!'

Scarron said, 'I shall pray for your soul.'

Wyatt said, 'Haw. Thanks very much.' He glowered, tossed the equipment to the priest, and scrambled into the forward cockpit. Scarron found a seat belt and decided he had better buckle it. The engine roared, and for some seconds Scarron forgot why he was there; his heart raced, and as the plane jolted forward he prickled in excitement; as they left the ground he marvelled at their power; and as they rose above the forest he knew

151

why the gods had lived on Olympus – why his own God ruled from beyond the stars. And when he first saw a moving Haitian, a thousand feet below, he held his breath, turned to gaze into the westering sun, and shocked himself with a heresy: if man could invent the flying machine, he could also invent God. The miracle of flight was perhaps more complex than the miracle at Cana.

Caroline Barbour. He prayed for yet another miracle.

Descending, he was queasy: Wyatt took them down in a series of swings, a little left and a little right and the nose low, surely that could not be right, surely they should be level, but no, and Scarron quelled nausea; finally they touched, bounced, settled, ran. They came to a halt. Wyatt gestured rudely with a thumb: out. Father Scarron divested himself of helmet and goggles – a moment's vision, the angel Gabriel in helmet and goggles, the Annunciation – and barely reached the ground before Wyatt whirled the Jenny, taxied to the chocks, and cut the engine.

They sat in the old plantation house and examined the map as if seeking clues: Father Scarron, Healy, McAllister, Dillingham, Neubauer, Dillingham's platoon sergeant Carnahan. 'There are ten thousand Haitians who know where he is,' McAllister said.

'The colonel's offered a reward,' Healy said. 'Everybody in Haiti knows about that by now.'

'A reward is the best way,' Scarron told them. 'I hate to say that but it's true. And if you find him?'

'Then comes the hard part. We're not authorized to make any exchanges, promises or payments. We *are* authorized to forget the whole matter if Miss Barbour is returned safe and sound.'

'It sounds so simple.'

'I know, I know,' Healy said. 'Wheels within wheels and mysteries within mysteries. Things go on here that no white man can comprehend.'

'I'm riding in with you,' McAllister said. 'I'll desert if I have to.'

'Good of you to give notice,' Healy said.

'First we have to find him,' Scarron said. 'If I rode into the hills, they would all pass the word, and Martel would send for me.'

'Yes. Wyatt says there's been traffic in the hills, groups on the trail east of here.'

A sharp double rap: Private Clancy called, 'Sir! Captain Healy, sir!'

'What is it, Clancy? Come in.'

Clancy braced and said, 'It's that Lafayette, sir. He says he has a thing to tell you.'

Healy said, 'Very good, Clancy. Send him in.'

Scarron asked, 'Lafayette?'

'A nickname,' McAllister said. 'He's the yard-boy.'

The yard-boy stepped into the room and halted; he bobbed a half-bow and said, 'Mon Capitaine.'

Healy said, 'What is it now, Lafayette?'

Lafayette was staring at the priest; he crossed himself and said, 'Mon père!'

Scarron said, 'B'jou, mon fils.'

Lafayette turned to Healy. 'Moins hear more news, mon Capitaine.'

Healy said, 'What is it, then?'

'Moins hear where is Martel,' the yard-boy said.

Now the Marines stared.

'Well, why don't you tell us?' Healy said.

Lafayette waited.

Healy exploded, then calmed himself. 'Goddam it, Lafayette, you'll have your reward, I told you that many a time. Now out with it!'

'It say,' Lafayette began, and started again. 'It say he bring his people one village, for vodun and talk about la guerre. Village is call Deux Rochers.'

'For Christ's sake,' Healy said. 'Where Gunny got it. Tell us again, Mac.'

'A rough approach, a ford. Then up a wooded hill. Stream runs through it. The village is the high ground and there's no easy way up, it's all forest. Jesus, we left them cloth and seed and every damn thing.'

Father Scarron said, 'You must not assume that the villagers love Martel. One day they cheer their liberators, not even sure what the word means; next day they weave spells to kill these bandits and chicken thieves.'

Healy said, 'But they're all black, saving your

presence, Father, and we're all white. Lafayette: what else?'

'It say,' Lafayette repeated, 'white Caco have her.'

'I knew there was a renegade!' Healy said. 'And a damn fine soldier the bastard is. By God, I knew it!'

Father Scarron was mystified: most of Haiti had heard rumours, yet this news amazed the Americans.

McAllister said, 'A white man.'

And now Scarron wondered: was the lieutenant angry or relieved?

'Father Scarron,' Healy asked, 'do you know where this Deux Rochers is?'

'No; but I can read a map.'

'I know where it is,' McAllister said. 'I'll take him in.'

'You'll do what I tell you,' Healy said.

'I resign,' McAllister said. 'I have no mufti but I'll strip off my insignia if you want that.'

Healy said, 'Lafayette: you go now. I'll see you later.'

The yard-boy backed out.

'I'd like to leave in the morning,' Scarron said.

'I'd like to leave tonight,' McAllister said.

'We can't do that,' Scarron said. 'Two riders in the dark are fair game. In daylight they'll see I'm a priest.'

'McAllister is not going anywhere,' Healy said, 'unless I say so.'

'I just resigned.'

'Your resignation is not accepted. There's a war on. You're under arrest till dinnertime.'

At dinner Father Scarron said, 'We're officers in different armies; and a victory for you is a defeat for me.'

'Meaning,' Healy asked, 'that God is not on our side?'

'God takes no side in man's wars. Would you have him rejoice in mayhem and murder?'

'Both sides always claim him,' Dillingham said.

'I believe he is neutral,' Father Scarron said. 'We define him as omniscient because we want to believe that he cares about our hangnails and nosebleeds, and omnipotent so he can cure them. But his concerns may be more sublime. You have no chaplains here?'

'In Port-au-Prince,' Healy said. 'They come out Sundays. So you're doing this as a civilian? A friend?'

'No; as a priest too. But God is not a Marine.'

'And the Marines ain't gods,' Healy said. 'I admit that freely. But we do a job as hard as yours, and we think we're doing good like you do, and we trust our chain of command like you do.'

'But your task is not hopeless,' Scarron said. 'Mine is.'

'I believe that's heresy,' Healy said. 'Mac, you haven't eaten a damn thing all day.'

'You look like hell,' Dillingham said. 'You're

not *ready*. You're no use to us or her dead on your feet.'

McAllister said, 'I'm retired.'

Healy slammed a flat hand to the table. 'Goddam it, McAllister, you eat and sleep, hear me? That's an order. I just may have work for you, you stupid swabby. Didn't anybody ever tell you that a good Marine is more afraid of his officers than he is of the enemy? Jesus! The Academy! Every time.'

McAllister said, 'Well now,' and his face came alive.

Healy said, 'Got to protect the Panama Canal, don't we?'

'Absolutely,' said Dillingham.

'Got to improvise in unforeseen circumstances, don't we?'

'Absolutely,' said McAllister.

Healy said, 'Loyalty up, loyalty down.'

McAllister said, 'Pass me some of that steak, would you, and the yams?' He drew a copious breath and collared another bottle of beer.

Dillingham said, 'Hell, I'd go in there myself, Mac. You know that.'

The three officers seemed to bask. Seminarian, priest, Roman Catholic, Father Scarron was no stranger to solidarity. It filled the room, as if these three had taken a vow aloud. He saw them better now, and liked them better; and distrusted himself for it.

* * *

157

Father Scarron slept well, on a cot in what seemed to be the guest bedroom, upstairs; painted on his chamberpot was a bouquet of pink roses. In the morning he dressed nervously; more excitement. Quite a vocation, the priesthood, what with flying machines and pastoral calls upon guerrillas.

Furthermore, he was set to work before breakfast, and admired the Corps' efficiency. The men rarely looked him in the eye, but brought him a bedroll, rations, a canteen. Flanagan offered a short course in horsemanship; it was unnecessary, but Scarron let him teach, and afterwards said gravely, 'Thank you, my son. The blessing be yours.' Flanagan tried to hide his pleasure but could not; perhaps he thought he was now safe from harm.

Scarron chatted for a moment with the yard-boy Lafayette, who rejoiced obviously in his presence. 'And what is your real name?'

'Emilien Bonenfant, Father. Emilien-zézé.'

Too good to be true, like the farmer named Bonhomme or the sailor Delamer.

'A priest is holy,' Lafayette went on with grateful solemnity.

'Tell me,' asked the priest, 'do the Americans treat you well?'

Lafayette was enthusiastic.

'Would you like them to stay on?'

Lafayette's enthusiasm swelled, and so did Lafayette.

'Would you like to be house-boy to an American family?'

Lafayette sighed for joy.

So to him I am a blanc, Father Scarron concluded. 'God bless you,' he said.

The priest and the three officers made a substantial breakfast – banana fritters and mango jam, rivers of coffee – and Scarron noted that McAllister tucked away his share, sitting alert, gabbing away. And what had Healy told the lieutenant? Interesting. A plucky one, this captain. Mettlesome. The sun was just up, and a few grey clouds drifted; Scarron hoped that rain would not delay them. He had considered riding clothes, but his soutane was essential.

'You don't fly the Haitian flag,' he said to Healy. It was red and blue – the old tricolour with the white slashed away.

'We did for a while,' Healy said, 'but my boys fussed and grumbled and called it a heathen banner. Do you fly it in church?'

'Of course not.'

McAllister said, 'Maybe we ought to fly it again. Maybe we ought to show some respect for two Haitians doing our work for us. Ambassadors.'

'Father Scarron's an ambassador,' Healy said. 'Lafayette's only a gossip, with eight or ten wives and a few business operations on the side.'

'Some Catholic,' Dillingham said.

'In the hills of Haiti there is neither marriage nor giving in marriage,' said Father Scarron. 'Your

159

Lafayette may have a dozen irregular connections. But I make no doubt he cares for his children and treats his women with courtesy, as their other husbands do when Lafayette is not available. What is his real name, by the way?'

'Hell, I couldn't pronounce it if I knew it,' Healy said.

'I thought not,' said the priest, 'Well, your yard-boy is an illiterate peasant, but he is a man of many talents. He speaks three languages, you know.'

Dillingham asked, 'Which three is that?'

'Creole and French and English.'

'That's one up on me and Mac,' Healy said. 'I have some Spanish and Mac's French is pretty good. Dill here hardly even speaks English.'

Dillingham said, 'I learned a few words at the Naval Academy,' and even McAllister smiled.

Healy asked, 'How many have you, Father?'

'Four, with the Latin; and a smattering of Italian.'

'I just hope you talk Martel's language,' McAllister said.

'I did once,' Scarron said. 'And a priest matters to Martel's people.'

'You may not matter to that white Caco,' Healy said.

'Don't you worry about him,' McAllister said, 'Captain, I want to thank you. You're laying a hell of a lot on the line for me.'

'Not for you,' Healy said. 'For your lady. You just fetch her safe and sound, hear?'

'I'll do that,' McAllister said, and to the priest, 'Let's move out, shall we?'

Flanagan led their mounts to the dusty ground below the veranda. 'These are my own horses,' McAllister told the priest. 'As sturdy as any troopers anywhere.'

'Huge brawny beasts they are,' Scarron said.

Marines stood quietly in the baked company streets. The officers and priest shook hands all around. 'Good luck,' Dillingham said. One of the men echoed them, 'Good luck,' and the others took up the cry, then subsided.

Healy said, 'God be with you.'

'An invocation,' Scarron murmured. 'Yes. Trust in the Lord.'

'I trust in you,' McAllister said.

And so the two mounted and started off, side by side, a wild light in McAllister's eye, Father Scarron erect and confident in the saddle but doleful within.

8

Showers broke in mid-morning, and thickened to sheets of rain; the white Caco inverted his slung rifle, led their wagon off the trail and bedded it snuggly among mahoganies. He wrapped the rifle in a spare shirt from his bedroll. Above them the rain snapped and danced on flat glossy leaves. He unhitched the mule and stripped his horse, wincing in the effort; he tethered both and offered water to Caroline. The brim of his sombrero was gently curled, and collected rain, and spilled it as he busied himself.

Caroline said, 'I'm cold and wet and hungry.'

'Drink. It's rum.' He tossed her a second canteen, uncased and shiny.

She shivered. 'Can we build a fire?'

He did not speak, only continued housekeeping.

The rum seared; she perked up in time to catch the saddle-cloth he flung at her. 'Over your head,' he said, 'like a Spanish woman.'

'A fire would help,' she said.

'There's nothing to burn.'

'Let me help,' she said. 'Let me move, let me be warm.'

'Be drier under the wagon,' he said.

She drew the pistol from her waistband and waggled it.

'Mon Dieu, les poules,' he said. 'I want to be dry, is all. If I lean back against the off fore wheel and you lean back against the rear wheel we can be cosy and your maidenhead will be safe for a few minutes at least and you can talk your bloody head off.'

'I'd like to kill you now,' she said. 'I'd love to see you dead.'

'That's rude,' he said.

Beneath the leafy canopy rain trickled and spattered. It must be a pelting rain in the open, but they were snug here. 'You go in there first and settle,' she said, 'and set food and drink between us.'

'You give orders like your papa. Little lady colonel.'

'You're not human,' she said. 'You speak French like a Frenchman but you can't be French because you speak English like an American and you can't be American because you speak Creole like a Haitian. You look like a Spanish bandit and you carry guns and knives and you'll do anything for money. You came here so you could be a big shot and abuse the poor Haitians, and their women too. I suppose behind their backs you call them niggers.'

'By Christ!' he whispered; he stood tall in the rain, he loomed, his blue eyes flamed. 'What do you know about me? You don't know the first fucking thing about me, or Haiti either!'

The flung obscenity staggered her. She rallied: 'I know you're a brute.'

'Where I come from,' he said, 'I'm a nigger, and it's not the United States.'

'My God, you *are* mad.'

'Christ, you're a silly girl,' he said. 'Put the pistol away and scoot under that wagon.'

Discretion was now the better part of valour; Caroline scooted.

For an hour they listened to the rain, and her anger floated between them like a mist; also a vague shame. She had not excelled in virtue. When he spoke it was sudden, and frightened her: 'Going to leave the cart. You'll ride muleback.'

Muleback! For an instant she was the equestrienne, indignant; then she was grateful. Life was improving. Whatever befell them she would prefer muleback with a pistol to the bed of a cart, unarmed. 'Thank you,' she said. 'Not in this rain.'

'It will let up in five minutes or so,' he said. 'At that time I am going in the bushes, and you go too if you need to.'

'Such gallantry,' she said. 'Exquisite.'

'Shut your goddam mouth,' he said.

The noon sun shone, and to the east a pale moon was just rising; the sky was golden, but as they picked their way through the forest residual rain dripped from the trees, and tree frogs, refreshed, chorused and chimed their rhythmic thanks, a grand choir of croaks and peeps and snores. The man rode before, and Caroline admired his courage; she knew that she would not kill him, but he could not know it. Or could he? What did she know of him or Haiti?

'I suppose it really doesn't matter about the pistol,' she said.

'I want you to have it,' he said. 'And keep your eyes peeled. If some sniper kills me, you'll have half a chance, and at the worst you can blow your own brains out.'

A distant tambour chattered then, and another. 'There they go,' he said.

'What are they telling us?'

'Never learned,' he said. 'They don't tell whole stories. They just say "traveller" or "danger", or "voodoo", or "blanc". They learned the beat from tree frogs. You heard, after the rain?'

'Yes. It was just frogs.'

'You listen again after the next rain,' he said. 'Kee. Kee. Kee. Then some others come in a little higher, ba-*dee*, ba-*dee*, ba-*dee*. Then some big old grandpapas, ka-*chungg*. Then some little ones, ko-ko-ko-ko-ko-ko. Pretty soon they're all at it together like some damn orchestra, and it *works*. They stay in rhythm, and the whole hillside makes music, and there's nothing but the golden sunlight and the green hillside and the music. Can't tell me where music came from. It came from tree frogs, that's where. African tree frogs.'

There was a note in his voice that she had not heard before: enthusiasm, a boyish pomposity.

165

She cocked her head, curious and confused, but found no words.

Soon they rode out of the forest, and he paused. 'Hold up,' he said. She halted her mule, which seemed neither stubborn nor hostile, but mindless and contented.

'We'll ride just below the crests,' he said, 'as quiet as we can. That little fellow is out there somewhere, and so are plenty of others, spies and hungry outlaws and just plain hired hands, and we had best head straight for Martel.'

She nodded.

'By God,' he said, 'I shut you up. No advice? No complaints?' He shocked her by smiling. She could not deceive herself: it was a beautiful smile, healthy white teeth, tanned face, dark brows: she battled a powerful impulse to smile back. 'My name is Blanchard,' he added, pronouncing it in the American manner, 'Louis Paul Blanchard. Pleased to meet you, I'm sure, and thanks for the bandage.'

'What – what a long speech,' she said.

'I have plenty to say,' he told her.

On the slopes were many copses, scrawny cedars or luxuriant raintrees bunched in hollows. Blanchard was following a trail of sorts: a goat-path, perhaps. He had dug out a pair of binoculars, and halted often to scan the hillsides. Caroline grew quickly hot and tired, and was pleased when he too squinted uncomfortably at the high sun.

'Those raintrees,' he said. 'We'll take cover and spread a fine luncheon. Oysters and a cool glass of Chablis.'

Chablis. Well, God knew who or what he was; for the moment, rest and food mattered.

He used the binoculars. 'Nobody stirring,' he said. 'Haitians are a naturally smart people. No busy-busy in the noonday sun. You notice the drums just quit? And way, way off there,' he pointed, 'see that wisp of smoke? Lunchtime, like I said. All of Haiti shucking those oysters and pulling those corks.'

They were well into the cool shaded grove when he halted. He pointed: a round platform only six inches or so off the ground, with gourds and shrivelled sour apples and coconut husks and solid little unripe pawpaws lying jumbled, all somewhat eaten away by ants and birds and the ordained scavengers that kept nature clean.

'A Caco shrine,' he said. 'Look closer.'

Concealed in higher grass beside the small platform was a flat rock about a yard across. Caroline dismounted. On the rock were a handful of coffee beans, a snippet of red ribbon, a crude knife with a wooden haft, a goat's skull, and a little human head moulded of lead, with an aquiline nose and thin lips. It was unquestionably the head of a blanc, and the shrine proclaimed a desire to replace it with the genuine article.

Much subdued, Caroline led her mule away.

* * *

They chewed dried goat's meat, mealy breadfruit, and plantain. Like a man-about-town Blanchard mixed her a rum-and-water in his canteen cup, and himself alternated swigs from the two canteens. He began tentatively but gathered speed and anger: 'Cold! In winter Quebec is like an ice cap. Fields of snow and ice, a whole province of snow and ice and the sun no more help than a penny candle. Farmers go crazy and kill their wives and children. You slaughter hogs in the autumn because you won't be able to feed 'em, and they hang on their hooks like marble. Can't even butcher till May. So you go on up to Montreal, where you have half a chance, but half doesn't seem enough so you go farther, you cross over to Ottawa, and then you're *really* a nigger. A Frenchman can walk in and he's a goddam prince and goes to every soirée in town, but a French Canadian swabs out the toilets in some government office.'

'Even with two languages?' This *was* a picnic; she was drowsy. The pistol lay heavy in her lap.

'Haw! Anybody else, people be glad to hire him. Not a French Canadian. Damn British! Damn Americans! Call us Canucks. Goddam Canada'd be another goddam Scottish desert without us, kirk and work and skinny women. Well.' He swigged deeper. 'Maybe I would never have amounted to much. My father was a pig farmer and country butcher and I can read and write and figure but not much more, except kill. This is his knife. I can take a man's head off with it. He gave it to me when I went to war.'

'You were in France.'

'Yeh. They told me I wouldn't have to go overseas. That was September in fourteen. I was in England by October and France by February. You know what Wipers is?'

'Yes. Ypres, the town in Belgium. The battles.'

'Three of 'em. The first one was around October, November in fourteen so I missed that. But I am one of the few men alive who went through Wipers Two *and* Wipers Three, and I tell you we are *doomed*. I *know* that. Just about the time we finish dividing up the world, we'll finish killing each other off. Some pygmies come along in about five hundred years and scratch their heads and wonder.'

'But it's over,' she said reasonably.

'Oh boy,' he said. 'Are you smart! These Haitians know: they don't want any part of your boy friend.'

'He was in France too.'

'Oh yes. The Marines have landed. Did I ever tell you I met your father?'

'You met my . . .'

'Yeh. Goddam parade. Officers, a band.' He snorted, and his face fell sullen. He slugged at his clairin.

Caroline said carefully, 'I've heard your cough before. I'm sorry.'

'You're smarter than I thought,' he said. His

169

eyes smouldered. 'Yeh. I was with the Canadian Division. We were right in the middle of that Second Wipers. It was April fifteen. The bloody Hun, we were already calling him that, the bloody Hun used chlorine gas against the 2nd and 3rd Canadian brigades. We went crazy. We tried everything. Kerchiefs dipped in water. A lot of good that did. Smells like hell, thank God, so we had warning. We tried to hold our ground and some of us did but Christ that gas rolled in. There was a lot of Africans in the line too, I remember, Zouaves and maybe some Senegalese, three battalions I think, and they just looked around at each other and said "Jesus Christ, the white man" and they ran, and it's what I should have done too. Us niggers got to stick together. Those poor goddam exiles, left their women and their sunshine for a dollar a day to come and rot in the bloody rain in Belgium and this great thick smoke kills them by the barrel.'

'It wasn't only you.' Caroline was angry: Bobby was scarred, might have died. 'There were thousands of brave men who didn't quit the human race.'

'Hell, yes!' he fired back. 'You want figures? I'll never forget 'em. Second Wipers: casualties: two thousand one hundred and fifty officers, fifty-seven thousand other ranks. Dead: ten thousand five hundred. Just to go back and forth over a mile of useless ground and maybe level a few buildings seven or eight hundred years old. That's not counting cattle and old women who got in the way. Those ten thousand five hundred sure quit the human race.'

And now he had begun, there was no end to it. They rode on; he talked away. 'All the smart ones died. The smart tommies because they didn't know a damn thing about war, and the smart lieutenants because it was the honourable thing to do when you had family and were supposed to run the world.' They were riding from copse to copse, and in the valleys more smoke rose, and they saw a river; time quickened. And still he talked, his voice low. 'Everybody good got killed. They made a feast for the rats – fat, slimy rats and those beady eyes shining at you in the rain. That's what tore my guts out, that and the gas. All the strong ones and all the smart ones, and who the hell is left in charge? *Millions*, lady! *Ten fucking million!* You understand me? On both sides; blow off their heads and they all look alike. Canadians, English, French, Russians, Italians, and Austria-Hungary or whatever and those Serbos, and Aussies and New Zealanders and Gurkhas – *Gurkhas*, the best fucking fighters in the world but there is no way to use even a Gurkha when machine guns can crossfire. That's why the Haitians have won. It may take a generation but they've already won. They won it in Europe. And the Chinese and the Japanese and the Hindus have won. And I'm on their side. You understand now?'

For a moment she simply could not speak. 'My father – '

'Yeh! Your father!'

' – once said that it was as if we were sorry we ever gave up human sacrifice; as if we were afraid we'd offended the gods, and had to revive it every few years to be sure who we were.'

'Your father said that?'

She nodded.

'That's pretty good,' he said. 'I sure sacrificed my share. Anyway they put me in hospital and let me cough for a while, and fed me up. I was still dizzy and still coughing when they reclassified me for light duty, so I was an officer's batman in 1916, and he was stitched across so they gave me to another one, but I knew what "light duty" meant: it meant that when they ran short of meat they'd send me up to the line. Which they did in the spring of seventeen. I was a corporal then. And the first thing that happened was, we won a great battle. It was someplace called Messines and the generals were all laughing and popping champagne, and we took seven thousand prisoners. I was guarding a line of them, scrawniest goddam Boche you ever saw, and one of them started to cough and for all I know he's still coughing, and that started me to coughing and we just looked at each other, we knew what it was all right, and we didn't say a word but we were asking each other, this German just about my age, skinny as a rail, we were asking each other why we let these fuckers do it to us. He had crown princes and dukes sitting in clubs, his Wilhelms and Ottos, and I had French and Haig, generals and field marshals. All leather chairs and tobacco pipes, and britches and shiny boots, and us poor sons of bitches – Jesus Christ, woman! The whole of goddam Europe is gone, you understand? Your boy friend won't win here because he can't. The white man is *finished*, and he finished *himself.*'

His saddle creaked, and horse and mule reeked pleasantly in the humid afternoon air. Caroline was calm, a nurse again: some of this she had heard before, some of it she understood. And now she wondered if her world had in truth vanished, if Bobby's career and her father's conference, if horse farms and shipyards, if famine in China and the women's vote, were only illusory scraps and remnants, grace notes to stave off, for a few bars more, the end of the great dance of history; if they were all plunging even now down time's chute into a black void.

And yet as he railed he became more human; she wanted to embrace him like a sister and to murmur, 'It will all end well.' She turned in the saddle to see his face. His eyes were not cold now, but burned; he was glaring in fury at his past. Abruptly they went blank, and he whispered, 'Hush! Stop!'

They drew rein; she listened.

'Into the trees! Quick!'

They sought the densest scrub, dismounted, tethered the horse and mule. 'You stay by me and do what I say,' he whispered.

She had seen nothing, heard only the hot sigh and crackle of a tropical forest.

He led her forward until the brush thinned. They lay side by side looking out over the slope and the trail they had just left, and now she saw: perhaps half a mile to the south, rounding the morne, a small parade, a line of men, only four but their gait oddly regular. Field hands did not march in close order; for an insane moment her mind said *patrol!* and for another insane moment she was sorry.

Not four: five. The four were marching in lock step like men shackled together. Each had laid a hand on the shoulder of the man before him; only the leader's arms dangled. Ambling along behind was a foreman in white trousers, and now she heard what Blanchard must have heard long before: the foreman seemed to be singing, or counting cadence.

She turned to Blanchard. Their faces were close; neither spoke. Her hand clutched the revolver: when had she drawn it?

Then he said, 'Zombies. Big fellows. Redskin haircuts like the dockers in Gonaïves, or Martel.'

'Port-au-Prince too,' she said. She lay breathless in the heat, and the summery fragrance of the grassy earth they lay on. Zombies! – she was a girl again, frightened and excited, and here was a pistol in her hand, and a boy beside her. One, two, one, two, and the foreman chanting, and the sun slanting off the green morne, and the smell of Blanchard's khaki and Blanchard's sweat. An exhilaration rose in Caroline, of Haiti and herself all compound, of magic and mystery, of fear and love, of Blanchard and Bobby; for one impossible stupefying tick of time she was a goddess.

'The Marines are afraid of them,' Blanchard murmured. 'The Marines don't want to fight dead men, because you cannot kill dead men.'

'They're not dead,' Caroline said.

'No. I know them. They live where we're going.'

'Be glad they weren't Cacos,' he said, when they were riding again, 'and for God's sake keep your eyes open.'

'You were telling me about the end of the world.'

'Important news. That pistol.'

'Yes?'

'When did you draw it?'

'I don't remember. When – I think when I dismounted.'

'Pretty good,' he said. 'On n'est pas fille du colonel pour rien.'

'Ni Canuck,' she said.

He pondered that. 'Pretty smart, too.'

'The end of the world,' she reminded him.

'Yes. There was a hell of a lot of us wiped out, Canuck or not. We attacked all summer, one attack after another. You were in the war by then and we figured it would end. Some day it would end. All those Colonel Barbours would come over with all those divisions, all those men with blond hair, six foot two, two hundred pounds, drive a railroad spike with one hand, and clean up those Huns in to weeks. Oh, the rumours! The Russians would reinforce and attack. The Italians would reinforce and attack. Meanwhile I was a machine-gunner and they were starting to call it the Third Battle of Wipers. I remember for a few weeks I even felt *good*. I would kill some people and cough a while and tell myself we were winning. I might have killed a thousand men. You realize that? A thousand men? Over and over, over and over, five here and ten there with the machine gun, and I had a dozen feeders killed – you know what a feeder – yeh – but I wasn't even scratched. I was with the Second Canadian Division then. Poor bastards.'

'Hold up a minute,' he said. 'We need a drink. I talk too much.'

'I never heard a man talk that way,' Caroline said. 'They tell me what great men they are or how beautiful I am but they never show me how they hurt.'

'Water only,' Blanchard said. 'No rum till we bivouac.'

'They say water has no taste; but it takes on the taste of the day.'

176

'I can still taste French water,' he said, 'in the form of mud. That fall it rained forever.'

'I remember.'

'You were there.'

'Before my father.'

'You're proud of that.'

'I suppose I am.'

'Did your bit.'

'Yes,' she answered. 'Do you want me to be ashamed of it?'

'No,' he said. 'It was all a bloody costume party but there's nothing to be ashamed of. For colonels on down there's nothing to be ashamed of.'

He scanned the hillsides; they rode on; he was silent for a long stretch, as if the well were filling again. 'I haven't coughed,' he said. 'Sometimes I just think about those days and I cough. We ambushed a bunch of your boys a while back and I was certain I would cough. Lay there like an iron man holding it back.'

'Don't tell me that. Tell me more about France.'

'Belgium, remember? Poor little Belgium. Hell, I don't know. Maybe they deserved it. They killed about fifteen million niggers in the Congo. Anyway, it rained. The rain. Rain started to fall towards the end of October, and it was real rain, like the flood in the Bible, the whole battlefield, the whole damn country, a swamp, barrage and heavy rain and barrage and heavy rain and you could hardly take two steps. Mud jammed every goddam thing, every rifle and every machine gun, and if you threw a grenade it just made a noise like a duck and flung mud. I heard even the shelling was no use, nothing would *blast*, only explode mud. Well, that wasn't so true. I found out the hard way. It was *all* the hard way that week. The Germans used gas again. This time it was mustard gas. That smells like new-mown hay but we knew there was no new-mown hay in all that rain and mud, plenty of new-mown soldiers but no hay. We had the masks by then. I was scared: one more little whiff of gas, any gas, and that was it for old Blanchard. Jesus, I was scared. And then I was too busy to be scared or anything else. I was killing plenty of Germans again, I'll never know how many, and I don't care. After a while it was automatic, I might have been firing in my sleep, and what happened was, I forgot to retreat. They read out the citation later and it said, "With his loader held a salient for four hours and so on, enabling B Company to withdraw from crossfire and so on, and return to the attack on Passchendaele village." We said "Passiondale" and I couldn't even spell it. I didn't even know B Company were there. And then came a lot of poetry about valour and beyond the call of duty and all that.

'That was my last day, sometime the first week in November. We crawled through the mud and the rain and the barrage and it was like living in a swamp, what do you call it, amphibious, and sometimes I wasn't even sure what I was shooting at – ours? theirs? the French?

'And then I was hit. There was a great blast and I was floating. It felt like I was just drifting up there about a hundred feet, and I was deaf. I remember the quiet. And all of a sudden I was eating mud and there were six or eight of us sitting around, almost in a circle like, and one was French because there was a French helmet in the mud, also some German helmets with the spike sticking up on top like some little tree about to grow.

'But these people were in bad shape. You listen now, Miss Barbour, Miss colonel's daughter, Miss society girl. Some of them were just trunks. There was an arm, a foot, and several heads bashed and one in mint condition. But all these bodies were *sitting*. They were holding a meeting, or maybe waiting for a hot meal, and some of them had no heads and no arms and one of them was just a pair of legs. Then I saw a whole body. It was whole except the blast had popped it open. So the head and the shoulders and the hips and the feet were all attached, but the belly was open like a fresh flower, but it wasn't fresh and it was all shit-brown. And then there was that one fine head. It sat right up in the mud like a cabbage, but it was a head all right and complete. Hair, eyes, teeth, everything but eyeglasses, and there was some neck too, because it was wearing a necklace. I patted myself all over and took inventory and I was all there, and I said, "Hello, my friends. Mes amis, meine Freunde." They just sat there. After a while I crawled over to inspect that necklace, and it was all British insignia – regimental badges and buttons and officers' pips and some rings. Gold rings from fingers. Goddam Boche stole from corpses.

'I vomited for about half an hour, and coughed up my guts. There was about every part of the male human body on display like a butcher shop. Then I passed out. Our people took the village and a burial detail found me next day. I had a bad cold. Not even pneumonia. All that, and I caught cold. And I'm going to shut up now. I'm tired of talking and I'm tired of Martel and your goddam Marines and I'm even tired of you. Don't say one goddam word until we have a rum in our hand. And keep your eyes open.'

When the bloodshot western sky faded to pinks and purples, he led her into a gully and over the far lip to a grove of mahogany watered by a rivulet. They made camp without speaking, and when they were secure a silent Blanchard measured rum.

Caroline said, 'May I ask a question?'

He nodded.

'Have you a family here?'

He nodded again, and said, 'Very fine woman in town, and a younger woman in the village.'

'Two.'

180

'No need to hide them,' he said. 'Haiti is all right. Men and women both, no need to sneak around and tell a lot of lies and call it a cinq à sept. Here you go. Don't spill.'

'Here's to valour,' she said.

'Yeh,' he said.

'What sort of medal did they give you?'

'Never mind that,' he said. 'I was so goddam ruined I never got it till January, and that was the last straw, that little bit of ribbon, that was the end, I left the next day and never looked back. I brought civilian clothes and walked south. I'm a Frenchie so the farmers took me on their wagons – hell of a lot they cared if I was a deserter, they knew their country was finished, sold, bleeding to death. This was nineteen-eighteen, remember. *Four years* of killing.'

'Less than two years ago,' she said. 'You're still killing.'

'It's my trade now,' he said. 'The only one I know. South of Bordeaux they didn't care a damn about the war – they were selling everything they could grow, at good wartime prices. They lost sons, they cared about that, and they cursed all those great men and treated me right. I had some money on me, my pay that there was no good way to spend and some that I won gambling, so I bought a carte d'identité and went over the mountains with smugglers and there I was a Frenchman on vacation in Spain. For some reason the Span-

181

iards were rude to the French so I crossed over into Portugal, fine country, and found a map of the world and made up my mind: warm, French-speaking, and no more lords of the world. No more white folks. Africa was too big. Haiti looked good and then I heard there was a bonus: I could find employment. I found it. I like it. And here we are.'

'Here we are,' she repeated. 'And where are we going?'

'A village,' he said. 'We'll be there soon.'

'Soon!'

'Yes. And listen: in Martel's village you're my woman. For your own good.'

'But you have one.'

'Well then I'll have two.'

'But you're selling me.'

'Shut up,' he said. 'That was then. This is now.'

'We can run for it,' she said. 'We can make it to the Marines. We can – '

'Shut up,' he said.

Sleep came hard: tomorrow! Louis Paul Blanchard. With his lungs and his bad dreams. A waste! With his sombrero and his slaughtering knife. With his easy manner and his man's ways, and the deep lesion, yet the truth of him too. And he would sell her or take her – yet here she lay with his pistol. Shoot him tonight?

And then? Go where? Shoot every stranger until only one cartridge remained?

In the moonlight he lay, eyes open; she saw the

rise and fall of his chest. No. She would not shoot Blanchard. What did his friends call him? Lou? Frenchie?

But of course: he had no friends.

In the night his kiss awoke her, and she was all sleep and love, dream and desire, and she clung to his face and drank deeply of the kiss; heat surged, and her breasts yearned, ached, and then she panicked and chose to be clever and to flee, drowsily murmuring, 'Bobby!'

Blanchard said, 'Liar.'

9

Scarron and McAllister rode without conversation that first morning. Crossing the open plain they heard drums chatter and watched muggy clouds scud slowly in from the southeast. McAllister worried about the priest, and glanced across to be sure that Scarron was not seated badly, or keeping too taut a rein, or sweating uncomfortably. Scarron detected those motherly concerns, and rode with nonchalant grace. These troopers were more amenable than Irish hunters.

Shortly they were riding through rain, less together than ever, as if McAllister's broad-brimmed olive-drab campaign hat and Scarron's broad-brimmed weathered straw hat marked two small independent territories. The plain was unsheltered but grassy, and they were spared bogs and quicksands. McAllister urged the pace, but the priest ignored him, and the lieutenant was forced to slow.

The wind backed, the rain slacked, and soon the skies were brighter. They approached the foothills, and McAllister led them to a brooklet, where they dismounted and stretched, and tore hungrily at ham sandwiches, and made small talk, pausing often to heed the garrulous drums.

'Your derrière hurt?'

'Not at all. I've hunted, you know.'

'Not in a cassock.'

'A soutane.'

'What's the difference?'

'None, really. Soutane in French. Listen: it occurred to me: will that Wyatt come searching? It would not help.'

'No. Healy will warn him off. We're on our own.'

They were gazing out over the plain, a fine prospect, some green gleaming now as the sun burned through, and patches of stunted maize, and the hills beyond; and the miraculous frigate birds, miles inland, soaring free, above all earthly sorrow. The drums beat more lazily, but rested seldom.

McAllister said, 'Tell me about Martel. Who he is and what he is and so forth.'

Scarron said, 'Tell me about Healy.'

McAllister observed the frigate birds. Man-o'-war birds. 'What is it you want to know?'

'He was exhilarated, and found work for you. What was it?'

McAllister swigged at his canteen, then topped it off in the brooklet.

Scarron said, 'Will you tell me?'

McAllister said, 'Yes. I'll tell you.' He replaced his canteen in its cloth case and sat comfortably, crossing his legs Indian-fashion. Scarron brushed at crumbs. McAllister went on, 'He ordered me to kill Martel if I could.'

'Would you do it?'

McAllister said, 'And be cut down on the spot? He was only creating a mission, for the record.'

'Would you do it?'

McAllister said, 'Do you sometimes feel that you're living in two worlds and don't quite believe in either of them?'

Scarron said, 'Constantly.'

'Failing that, he said I must bring back intelligence. Do you want his exact words?'

'Captain Healy's exact words are worth hearing.'

'He said, "I'm not sending you after any girl, is that clear?" Any girl! Then he said, "You better come back with *something* or they'll have my ass. And for Christ's sake do come back."'

Scarron said, 'Amen. Would you do it?'

McAllister looked him in the eye and said, 'Trust me.'

Scarron said, 'Trust you! When I can't trust myself? I came very close to violating the secrecy of the confessional.'

'And a damn good thing!' McAllister said. 'Does your God want her out there,' and his voice rose a notch, 'tied up and beaten, or raped?'

'We never know what God wants.'

'Save that for Sunday school,' McAllister said. He collected the debris of their picnic.

'Look at me, man,' Scarron said. 'I am a black Haitian priest doing white man's dirty work.'

'Stop whining, Father. Let's move on. You're black,' and McAllister's impatience ran off with him, 'and so is Martel, and so's His Excellency in Port-au-Prince. You're not doing white man's dirty work: if Healy's right you're helping us hunt down a mad white man. Oh, what the hell, Father, nobody makes war on women and children!' They rose and approached the horses. 'I'll be just as frank and tell you I wouldn't care who won if we could bring my girl out safe, and I wouldn't care even then except that I am a Marine and under orders. Tell you the truth, I don't believe there's a man in my outfit gives a damn who runs Haiti, or wouldn't fight just as hard if our orders were to back Martel.'

'You'll meet him soon,' Scarron said. 'Tell him that.'

'I may do just that,' McAllister said. 'Now tell me about him.'

Scarron obliged him as they rode, sketching the boy and painting the man in vivid oils. Charlemagne Masséna Martel stood six feet three, weighed two hundred pounds, was coal-black and shaved his head but for a hedge down the middle in the old Dahomeyan manner. He wore cotton trousers narrow in the leg and his muscular thighs bulged. Sometimes he wore a loose cotton shirt with a neckerchief, a red-and-white American bandanna, and when he was not barefoot he wore wooden clogs with a thong.

He had been arrested in the summer of 1918 and sentenced to five years' hard labour for complicity in a Caco raid on a gendarmerie outside Hinche. He did not admit his complicity; he affirmed it. He had became an outlaw to fight slavery, which was now called the corvée and consisted of forced labour on the roads, only a few days each year but forced, and the period sometimes extended without notice, the labour in lieu of taxes and other charges, some reasonable but most not. At any rate it was the Americans who enforced the corvée; how could a free Haitian tolerate that?

Because he was literate and fiery, and had studied with the white Jesuits, and once visited France, he was set to street-sweeping in Cap-Haïtien on the northern coast, with an armed policeman on guard at all times. This was to humiliate him. The authorities, including various Excellencies in Port-au-Prince, were sharply opposed by a canny and dangerous politician in the north called Fleury who was Martel's friend; they assumed that the townspeople would mock the prisoner and through him Fleury. Rumour urged the citizens to dump their garbage in Martel's path.

They did no such thing. They lined the streets in silence and directed their sullen hatred at the policeman, who was called a chasseur or hunter. The word also meant lackey. Many of the spectators flung powders in his direction, and some brought small bowls and sat grinding at invisible ingredients. Others chanted softly, sly of eye.

Martel was direct, logical and fluent. The combination of popular disapproval, open witchcraft and Martel's persistent eloquence converted the chasseur, who in September joined him in flight to the mountains, where Martel rallied a band of guerrillas and led them south, towards the centre of Haiti. Less than a month later, the corvée was abolished. Martel laughed. For him history was the French Revolution, Napoleon and several dozen Haitian tyrants: he knew how often kings made concessions a day late.

He had three thousand followers, but let the world believe that there were five thousand, ten, a whole nation ready to rise. Of the three thousand, perhaps three hundred were experienced bandits. The rest were farmers, wood gatherers, river fishermen, goatherds, village distillers − men and women and a number of growing children for whom war was a complicated new recreation.

Some of his people were giants like himself, some grandmothers, some crafty runts, some born to shopkeeping families with an impressive income like $100 a year, and some thieves, pimps, and dedicated troublemakers. Within fifty miles of Deux Rochers he had a thousand part-time rebels. He could dress as a beggar, walk stooped through a village at dusk, and tell by the look on a face or the hint of a swagger that this was his man, his woman. What he could not do was mass a well-drilled army. An ancient paradox, an ancient flaw: good guerrillas made bad regiments, and so often today's revolution became tomorrow's tyranny.

Martel stood tall among his bad regiments and surly civilians; concealed his doubts and fears and angers; acted the shrewd, revered patriot, hated by the rich, beloved by the poor. His principal woman was called Zan Rousse, which meant Susanna the redhead. There were always three or four others; he was a man of large appetites practising a dangerous trade, and he was a man who knew the value of trappings. He often carried a bullwhip: it evoked the enemy, and roused his people to useful anger.

He had said often that he wanted only to raise a family, and to love his neighbour. This was appreciated as high good humour.

Later the two entered the forest, and to the priest it was Eden: fruit and flower, dove and wild goat, gnarled cedar and broadleaf — here, he said in Irish, the hand of man has never set foot. The distant drumbeats were muffled. He meditated on Martel, struggling for this primeval kingdom. How long since their last boyish impassioned talk? Twenty years? He calculated: fifteen, sixteen. Now and than a greeting, via some third party. Martel had won battles, killed, lost friends, women; this would be another Martel entirely. A Martel who saw Caroline Barbour as plunder.

Here in the shadowy forest, the priest led the way: the perils, if any, lay hidden, and the soutane was their shield. They chattered, tried to laugh and be boisterous; they must travel openly. But not dawdle, and McAllister complained: 'You're poking along.'

'You're nervous,' Scarron said. 'Shall we race through the forest, and be taken and bound and flung in a hut while messages limp back and forth?'

'I want to ride my horse into the ground,' McAllister said, 'and I see Martel behind every tree, and I wonder if Healy is playing tricks and planning an attack right behind us, and I wonder if Lafayette is a Caco, and I wonder if Caroline is dead.'

'Stop it now,' Scarron said. 'Caroline is worth more unharmed.'

'My men can make ready for a week's patrol in half an hour. And you poke along.'

Scarron said, 'You won't see Martel at all without me. Besides, you're dressed for this and I'm not. I am not one of your hussars. Respect for the cloth, please.'

'Yes. You're right. Are you really immune? Safe? You're like some good luck charm.'

'No one will fire upon us. These more remote Haitians may go a year without a visit from a priest. My own predecessor administered the last rites, post mortem, to seventeen of twenty-eight villagers struck down by a bloating disease never identified – high fever, watery bowels, fire in the bones and joints. They had not seen a doctor or a priest for eighteen months. He described it in writing for a medical magazine in Paris. The eleven survivors were emaciated but Catholic, and they wept when he offered Mass. They then sang to Papa Legba, and sacrificed a hen.'

'As Dillingham says, some Catholics.'

'It is perfectly natural. You Protestants seem to believe in at most one God, but saints and angels are more than abstract here; they are the spirits of fire and storm, rain and tree, yam and drought.'

'Our saints lived or died for the faith,' McAllister said.

'Ours are far more versatile,' Scarron assured him. 'There is even a sort of hermaphroditic oracle who negotiates with the dead, and the lord of the graveyard is called Baron Saturday.'

On the second day they emerged from the forest and crossed more plain; and in mid-afternoon they reached a broad stream and a ford that McAllister knew well. Halfway across they were halted by one rifle shot; the round whizzed by them, and the report echoed off the hillside. On the far bank there suddenly stood two armed men, naked to the waist, ouanga bags dangling.

No one stirred. McAllister's mount strained to drink. McAllister hauled roughly on the reins and called, 'Is the blanche here?'

One said, 'No blanche.'

McAllister said, 'Christ. Do you know where she is?'

The other said, 'No.'

Scarron told the men, 'Martel is my old friend.'

They were much alike, these two sentries, ragged but bright-eyed. One said, 'You must give the password.'

'I'm afraid I don't know the password,' Scarron said. 'But Martel will be angry if you turn me away.'

McAllister interrupted: 'Last month it was "Ouvri chemin".'

Scarron said, 'Oho.'

'Open the way?' McAllister asked.

'Yes. It's from an incantation in vodun.'

The second guerrilla said, 'Your guide will be back in a little moment.'

'Guide?'

'We saw you an hour ago,' the man said, 'and watched you, and when we saw that you were a priest, Oreste ran up the hill for orders.'

'Then we may cross? My horse is restless here.'

'Cross. And listen, blanc, keep your hands off your weapons.'

McAllister said, 'I think our guide should carry them — Oreste, is it? Martel would call it good soldiering.'

The sentry made moon eyes.

But Scarron saw the reluctance, the disquiet, when Oreste returned and McAllister disarmed himself; rifle, pistol, bayonet.

* * *

193

'My God, what a mob,' McAllister said. 'Last time there were a couple of dozen women and a swarm of kids.'

Their armed escort was hostile and silent; six men; Oreste bore McAllister's arms proudly.

Outside each hut men and women stared, and most of the men held weapons. Children clung to the women. The men lounged and spat. On the green lay crates; on a crate lay a goat, chewing the cud.

Scarron sketched a sign of the cross, and a subdued cheer arose. 'B'jou mon père!'

'B'jou mes enfants, and God bless you all!' He led McAllister to the houmfort and crossed himself again before the crucifix-cum-serpent.

As if in answer, Martel emerged. He was shirtless and barefoot. He wore a conical straw hat and a pair of white cotton trousers, cut off just below the knee. In his right hand he carried a coiled bullwhip.

Immediate silence: Martel measured McAllister, and tried obviously to stare him down; McAllister held his ground. Martel looked for the Marine's weapons, frowned, glanced at Oreste. His brows shot up, and he shifted his attention to Scarron, who was impressed again by the man's sheer size: tall, massive, well-fed now and hard.

'Ti-Jean!' Martel barked. 'A ghost from the past! Not yet unfrocked, hey? You had better tell me what the devil is going on, and introduce me to your foolish friend.' And copiously, deliberately, he hawked and spat, and said to McAllister, 'B'jou, macaque!' The villagers seemed to exhale one sweeping musical sigh.

McAllister said, 'That means "monkey", I believe.'

Martel said, 'Yes. One stage above "Marine".'

Scarron laid a hand on McAllister's shoulder.

McAllister said, 'Never mind. We're not waging war today. Call me what you want.'

Martel called out, 'Everybody! Look at this blanc! This servant! This paid killer!'

McAllister reddened. The priest asked Martel, 'You've heard about the blanche?'

'Of course I've heard. It was done at my order.'

Scarron knew immediately that the man was lying: the tone was that of a confessant inventing sins.

McAllister said, 'And you call me – ' but did not finish. 'Where is she?'

Martel slapped the bullwhip against his thigh. 'I have no idea. On her way here, I should think. Now: I'm placing you under close arrest. You will confine yourself to the hut. Armed men will guard you and women will tend to your needs. Consider your sins, improve your Creole. This is the Haiti no blanc knows. Travel broadens one.'

'The seed corn,' McAllister said, 'and the bolts of cloth: my men and I brought those to the village. You ambushed us, and killed a boy.'

'We killed a killer,' Martel said. 'The ambush was not my idea, but it was a good one. We never invited you. Now go away, Lieutenant. My social graces are rusty.'

'For the love of God, can you help?' McAllister pressed him. 'Will you take me instead? *What can I do?*'

'Nothing,' said Martel. 'I have no idea where she is, and Blanchard is a cold man. Unpredictable. He may have her on a ship, or across the border in San Domingo, or harnessed to a mill-wheel in a village.'

'Blanchard! Who's Blanchard?'

Martel snickered: 'He is the white Caco, my chief of staff and French poodle. You will occupy his hut. Now leave me. You understand: I cannot like you.'

'Blanchard!' McAllister said. 'French! Not a deserter?'

'He came from Europe,' Martel said, 'and his old-fashioned French is more formal than mine.' He dismissed the blanc.

Two guards grasped McAllister, each by an arm.

'No need for that,' McAllister said.

'You're a prisoner,' Martel said.

McAllister studied him. 'I'll do anything. Remember that.'

Again Martel gestured; the guards marched off with the blanc.

'He is not a bad man,' Scarron said. 'He is in fact a rather good man.'

Martel said, 'Oh well, *you*.'

* * *

The two Haitians strolled the village. 'You will say a Mass,' Martel assured him. 'Now: who else is on the way? What have the Americans planned for me?'

Scarron noted the preponderance of men over women, perhaps three to one, and both sexes a mixed bag, all sizes and shapes and degrees of beauty. Some of the men wore felt hats and some cloth caps, and one or two campaign hats, and Scarron saw more than one Marine Corps globe-and-anchor; and some were bareheaded, and many sported a scarlet token. Some looked like brave soldiers and some looked altogether evil, shifty-eyed and sullen, half-drunk. Many strutted armed – ancient rifles or modern, pistols, daggers and bayonets and cutlasses. The men paraded with their weapons while the women worked. 'No one else is coming,' he said. 'It is only he and I, and we only want the woman.'

'Ah! A wistful note! Has the priest met the beast within?'

'I met him years ago,' Scarron said, 'and slew him. Charlot! Charlot! You are not a man for molestations, for atrocities, for dismal, ugly, venial sins!'

Martel rambled, and Scarron heard the qualms, the note of underlying apprehension. He had expected a god, a massive statue in ebony, but here was a human being struggling against doubt, restive, loquacious. 'My old Ti-Jean! How long has

197

it been? You keep low company, my friend. Cabinet ministers. American officers. We are planning a Petro service, you know, a fine wholesome blood sacrifice to raise our spirits. And to shock our old friend the priest. Perhaps in a day or two? Men and women have been pouring in from everywhere, whole families. They come from fifty miles away – they come for the vodun and the rum and the feasting but they come for God too, and for Martel, and for a raid or two, hey? They swarm in, and pray to the two great boulders, and ask permission to drink and bathe. They bring a kerchief full of beans and a bag of ground maize. Deux Rochers can hardly accommodate them. They stake claims and tear down patches of young forest and braid together little huts. What shall we sacrifice? A goat? A bull? Your Marine? Wait till you see our Petro girl. You must purify us next day. Look here: see these stones? Deux Rochers is what remains of a plantation built in seventeen seventy-two by slave labour.'

Scarron saw the ruins, the cornerstones exposed now and weathered; they served as querns or chopping-blocks. There remained curious boundaries and scraps of stone wall. Beyond the village, sloping down in all directions, stood true forest, dense stands of mahogany uncut for a century save as casual village need arose, with here and there a field of cane patiently expanding, season by season over that same century.

A Petro service. He was not shocked. They

would kill a bull and slice him up and it was a way to share the wealth. It was rather Martel who shocked him, volatile, fizzy, chattering away, a man approaching some inner limit. No ebony god at all, Martel was subdued and melancholy over rum and beancake: 'I have not enjoyed myself. It is a barbarous life. I was once a Catholic, remember. I should like to win my war and be a family man like Toussaint.'

Scarron said, 'The colonel told me you should have been an officer in the gendarmarie.'

'He did, hey? And what did you tell him?'

'You know what I told him. I was quite cold.'

'Cold. Do you remember how you used to go on about winter? You were a famous bore about winter.'

'Was I indeed?'

'Oh yes. You were persuaded – against your will, you said, by the weight of history, you said – that winter, the threat of death by freezing and starving, made men think and do. Made them build houses and store foods and sew thick garments and keep promises.'

'Was I wrong?'

Martel shrugged. 'Schoolboy philosophies. Look at our people! Heirs to glory, survivors of unutterable brutality, and now worse than peasants. Tribesmen, worshipping reptiles and storms. Their reality is all superstition.'

'How tactless, to a priest.'

'They are barely acquainted with the wheel,'

Martel said stubbornly, 'and they love me for my bullwhip, and do you know what they want from me? They want me to lead them to a kind of heaven: a place full of fat fish and livestock, mahogany and cassava, and no cities. By God, maybe the Americans *should* win!'

'Toothpaste and telephones?'

'Yes, and manners and sanitation – no! To this village good manners are sacred, and before my armies trooped in it was a clean little spot, eternal. No, by God, your winter is a delusion, the white man's boast. The Egyptians never knew winter. They wove cloth-of-gold and wrote books and built the pyramids.'

'With slaves.'

'Quick as ever, Ti-Jean. Yes. With slaves. The blood of generations poured into monuments to superstition.'

'Like our Citadelle.'

'You will provoke me. You're worse than a Jesuit.'

And later: 'I have no idea where the woman is. My Caco blanc, my trained house-boy,' and Scarron was startled by the hot current of hatred, 'has doubtless ravished her and will bring her to me as an offering.'

'He fears you so?'

'Of course he fears me! He's a killer but a thinker, my Caco blanc. All Frenchmen are thinkers, hey? With their *cogito* and their Rights of

200

Man. Already I know his mind: he brings me a gift, so I will owe him one. As long as I hold that girl, the Marines will be immobilized. They will not dare attack. I shall have her seen at various spots, and rumoured at others. I tell you, he is a smart bugger. A tough son of a bitch, and I don't like him any more than I like your lieutenant, but he is a smart bugger. In return for this dangerous favour he will ask to mount a general offensive. That is what I want; but it must seem his idea.'

'History will snicker. "Martel maintained power by the judicious use of helpless women."'

'You provoke me again. Listen: I am fighting a war, and I have my majors and my captains; but I see beyond the war, and they do not. I want to *govern*, and all I can do is skirmish. I need a city. A large town or city to man and hold. Without that I cannot coordinate, you understand? I use drums! runners! smoke signals! Nonsense, in modern war! And I need an offensive – I want to strike at every major gendarmerie in central Haiti, and let the Marines react in all directions, with the whole countryside lying in ambush. And soon! Men are falling sick. Fevers, fluxes, epidemics!'

'Like the yellow fever that destroyed the French.'

'Never!' Martel roared. '*We* did!' And then, 'I should never have let you ford that stream. In my whole life no one ever angered me as much or as quickly as you always do. From the very start.'

Scarron told him, 'We are not too different, you and I.'

Martel groaned. 'I knew you would say that. Let's go visit your white friend, before you drive me crazy.'

But he changed his mind, and sent Scarron alone. 'I'll see him tomorrow. I'll send for him.' The priest blessed two armed guards and found McAllister fallen upon luxury and corruption. In Blanchard's hut were crackling pallets stuffed with straw, and bowls, coconut halves, with lighted wicks floating on palm oil. In corners or on low platforms were a human skull, a pair of goat horns, and three or four tunics, red, blue, white. And a hammer, a small drum and a larger drum, a wooden snake, and a heap of small skin bags – ouanga bags to be. Goatskin, perhaps mole-skin, snakeskin.

McAllister was drinking from his canteen cup, and waved it mournfully. 'Not a word about Caroline, and they've forced rum on me. An old friend, an old woman in a blue tunic. She remembered me.'

'Martel did not lie: he has no idea where Caroline is. I'll take a drop.'

'There's your gear. This stone jug is rum. At the moment I am very damn depressed. Un vrai cafard.'

Scarron poured, added water, stirred with his index finger. 'Me too. Hope deferred maketh the heart sick. On the other hand it's late in the day

202

and we're tired, and hope makes a good breakfast but a bad supper. Martel is a worried man, I can tell you that much. He did not order the abduction and he does not like this Blanchard and he is rather tired of war. He has other educations he would rather make use of. A hell of a day, you're right, a hell of a day. Listen, my boy – '

'Your what?'

'Lieutenant.'

'That's all right,' McAllister said. ' "Boy" will do fine. I'm not much of a hero today.'

'I was only going to suggest that you drink up and pour another. They'll send in food, and take us to the stream, but we cannot hurry matters.'

'I asked her if the women made the rum and she said no, the men and the zombies. Did you see any zombies?'

'No. The rum is good. They add guavaberries.'

'That's wonderful,' McAllister said. 'How broadening is travel, as the man said. Maman speaks slowly and I understand her. She asked if I needed a woman.'

'Easy does it. Drink up.'

'Dutch courage?'

'No. You'll sleep better.'

Later the old woman returned, and she was not alone. Scarron and McAllister stared; the priest drew a deep breath, and smiled to see the war on McAllister's face. With the old woman was a very young woman wearing only a breech-clout. It was obvious that the lieutenant found her disturbing:

his lips parted, his expression was suddenly brutish, he could not take his wide eyes from her body. The priest found her beautiful, either more or less than human: frizzy hair like a helmet on the round head, the nose of no race, the lips voluptuous, the neck and shoulders framing flawless breasts. Obscure dangers singed him, too sharp and transient to be the monk's old bane, morose delectation. Her waist was slim and supple, her motion was dance, her buttocks were high and round, her thigh was long, her calf was full. For a tremulous long moment he suffered the truth of lust, and almost gasped. He called upon Christ, and all was well.

'Belle ti, ça,' maman agreed. 'She is Faustine, the blanc's woman. Also the hen-girl at the Petro service, and the goat-girl and once the bullock-girl.'

Faustine spoke little, maman said, and was believed to inhabit another world, among the gods.

The two Haitian women served them goat chops and the inevitable beans and a bitter flat breadfruit cake. Maman chattered on: Faustine had gathered firewood as a child, and tended kids with a switch, and was fond of sucking at cane. She scrubbed the smaller vessels with sand. She worked fresh goatskins and pounded grain. She also crafted small snakes and birds and Christs on the cross, and sacred trees and suns and full moons and the horned goat. It was she who chanted and hummed the old invocations: prayers for rain, and for not too much rain, for the health of donkey's hoofs; for no sandstorms; for fecundity among the domestic animals, or for the immediate fertility of one; for the victory of a fighting cock; against invasion by the small people from the east.

And the charms and curses: against bellyache, sterility, pregnancy, cramps, rape; against murrain and the death of valuable beasts; against faithless men, labour pains, the police and the blancs; against smallpox and yellow fever. Against untimely marriage; for timely abortion. And more curses: to kill, to disquiet the freshly dead, to strike down a rival in love. And potions: for love or sleep or slow death.

McAllister said, 'My God.'

'The Haiti no blanc ever sees.'

McAllister said, 'I know so little about Haiti.'

'Does she rouse desire, this young one?'

'Oh yes,' McAllister said. 'I try not to lie to myself.'

Scarron inspected him again, this lord of the world, this blanc, the new hero, democrat-aristocrat, eternally youthful and not unintelligent. 'He is not a bad man. He is in fact a rather good man': yes. But history was made by bad men. Without Judas, where was Jesus? Or was Judas God's agent for good?

Who was the Judas here, he wondered, and who the Jesus.

Later the guards marched them to the stream and back, and McAllister stretched and groaned and yawned and cursed. Father Scarron whispered his evening prayers like a child, adding a fervent plea for Caroline; he felt less empty and more Christian in these pagan hills.

No woman came to the hut that night, and Martel himself woke them in the morning. Scarron struggled to the surface of a dream, and before he was properly awake heard the deep raging voice, 'You're in luck, Marine. That French macaque is on his way, and he has made his mistake, and he is all yours.'

10

Caroline and Blanchard rose to a fine clear yellow dawn. Blanchard was silent, Caroline sullen: new fears. Perhaps time should stop here, events never better, never worse, a safe eternity. Blanchard tended to the animals, patting his horse and murmuring, 'Sammy.' Finally he said, 'Hot coffee'd go nice about now.'

'Bacon and eggs,' she said. There might be awful journeys to come. Perhaps she would look back wistfully on her days with Blanchard.

'Won't be long,' he said. 'Can be done, you know, bacon and eggs. Mountain hog fattens easy here. Suckling pig one time: damn good. For now, plantain and water.'

'I'll live,' she said. Doves settled to peck at their scraps.

They were high in the hills, and half that morning they descended rolling ridges. It was a day full of doves: they cooed like little owls, oo-coo, oo-coo. Wood rats peered from the brush, unafraid, curious. Placid wisps of black smoke or white rose miles off — homes, farms.

Blanchard was all talked out. But what he had told her worked in her now, and spoiled even Paris. Bobby in the Tuileries, Bobby in the Bois, and the saucers and filtres and horse-cabs, and thanks to Blanchard it was all dying, the ashes of civilization settling like dirty snow on the great cities. Blanchard's lips pressing her own: she groaned in shame but the groan did not deceive her.

'Listen,' he said, 'I'll stick by you.'

'Thanks. My buddy.'

They paused for clairin and water. It was like the end of a season: over. The last petal. The first snow.

'I'd best have that pistol,' he said.

She passed it to him. She had killed a man! For three hours she had ridden these hills and that had not once crossed her mind. I have killed a man. She said it again: it was without real meaning.

Once in the lowlands they rode faster, across a patchy plain, dried grasses, stands of cane; mongooses fled, like great savage alien squirrels.

'I hope they come out to meet us,' Blanchard said. 'Every damn stand of trees looks like bandits.'

'How would they know?'

'They know.'

Yes: they knew everything. The tambours. The ambush at the ford. 'Blanchard,' she said.

'What?'

'Nothing. I never said your name before. Louis Paul Blanchard.'

'Caroleen Barbour.'

'Caroline.'

'Caroline,' he said comfortably. 'My girl Caroline.'

'What's your other one's name? Or the two.'

'In the village, Faustine. In town, never mind. The woman in town is my friend,' he said.

They rode, and the breeze died, and the sun lay heavy. Blanchard's eye roved, but the plain was deserted. 'There,' he said at last, and she saw a wooded morne, imposing, rising vast and bluff from the plain, a gentle humped range of mornes beyond it; she saw a darkish dazzle, a stream; miles yet to go.

The small Haitian sat across the fire from McAllister, and all four men swallowed hot coffee from wooden bowls. Women waited upon them, and one was the girl Faustine. The little man said, 'Fleury heard her crying out and went to the wagon. There was a scuffle and then a shot, oh it was loud, like thunder in the night, and I dashed for the bush and took cover. I heard them talking afterwards, the two blancs.'

The smoke of fresh fires hovered. Villagers hovered too, at a distance. The little man was filthy and red-eyed, and spoke through mouthfuls of sweet potato.

Martel spat into the flames. 'That fool Boniface!'

'Your friend,' Scarron said.

'My friend! To let Fleury's son die!'

'Fleury's son on the left hand.'

'So, a bastard. We are all bastards here. Fleury doted on the boy – boy! Already a man! They called him Gros-Cul because he chewed tobacco.'

McAllister did not understand.

Scarron said, 'It means rough-cut tobacco but also Fat Arse.'

'So I have no choice,' Martel said. 'Well, I don't mind seeing Blanchard dead but I thought Boniface was shrewder. Unless – no. Boniface is one of us. But to send the boy with Blanchard! The boy could read and write!'

'Blanshar,' the little fellow said. 'Brrr.'

McAllister asked him, 'Did you wait for morning?'

The Haitian squinted at this blanc; not at him, not quite; and said, 'I waited. I hid myself and waited and in the morning when the wagon was gone I went to see, and I found Gros-Cul.'

'The blanche,' McAllister said. 'Did you see her?'

'I did not.' To Martel the little man said, 'This is one of the blancs. Why do we parley with him?'

'He will be gone tonight,' Martel said, 'one way or another. Can you find Gros-Cul again?'

'Oh yes. He lies in the old valley Josselin, up the south slope.'

McAllister was reborn. Hope burned like a fever as the priest translated patiently from Creole. The little Haitian had blurted his tale ten times – he had told Martel, and the men, and the women, and the children, and other men, anyone who would listen, and now he sat bug-eyed before Martel while the priest murmured to the blanc. 'It might have been me,' the little man said.

'But it was Gros-Cul,' Martel said. 'And Blanchard is coming here. I want to know something, and I want you to think, and remember.'

'I am thinking,' the man said. 'I am remembering.'

'Then tell me if Blanchard knew who the boy was.' Tell me if he ever used Fleury's name.'

The man considered this in silence. They heard the snap of burning wood, the cry of a baby; in a nearby hut a bolt shot home – a guerrilla cleaning his weapon. 'He never used Fleury's name or my own. Not once did he say to him, "Fleury," or "Gros-Cul," or to me, "Ti-Tomas." Only "ou".'

'Good,' Martel said.

'Good,' McAllister said.

'Why good?' the priest asked.

McAllister and Martel spoke at once. Martel nodded, and McAllister went on: 'If he knew who the boy was, he'd head for the border. He didn't know, so he'll just come home.'

'Hired thugs,' Martel said. 'He thought they were hired thugs. It's the language he understands.'

'I'd like my weapons now,' McAllister said.

'You'll have them in time. The Marines have mutilated Cacos, you know.'

'And the Cacos have mutilated Marines.'

'Patience. Hours yet.'

211

'It feels like Sunday,' Scarron said. 'One of the sad Sundays.'

After this early coffee they dismissed Ti-Tomas. 'The sun barely risen,' Martel said. 'Hot meat this morning, hey? Chicken, I think. You,' he called, 'Faustine! Spit a chicken, with the little apples and the sea-salt and the plantain. You hear? You understand? Good. Do it now. I like that,' he told Scarron and McAllister. 'Let his woman cook for us.'

'If he didn't know who Gros-Cul was,' Scarron said, 'he is not so much at fault.'

'It is not a question of fault,' Martel said. 'Fleury is me and I am Fleury and no more need be said. I'd kill Blanchard myself but am being courteous to my enemy here, who has a prior claim. If the lieutenant misses, I do the job myself.'

'The lieutenant will not miss,' McAllister said.

'Bad enough to hurt Fleury,' Martel said. 'If I cannot show him Blanchard's body, God help me and all of us.'

McAllister said, 'We do it at the ford?'

'Certainly. He must come that way. The sentries are out now, and will report when they see him. We have every advantage at the ford.'

'I know all about the advantages,' McAllister said.

'I shall stand on the bank, and wave him welcome.'

'Is that usual?'

Martel said, 'No.'

212

'Perhaps it should all be as usual as possible.'

'Yes; perhaps the sentries will greet him. But I must see him dead. No more white Cacos.'

'About my weapons . . .'

'Shut up about your weapons! I cannot have you flaunting weapons. In my village no blanc carries a weapon.'

'Blanchard did.'

'No more. I will carry them to the ford; I will hand them to you myself. You must behave yourself, Lieutenant. My men have you always in their sights.'

'I'm your guest,' McAllister said. 'It is not my habit to shoot my hosts.'

'There are a number of dead Haitians who might contradict you.'

McAllister made no answer, but in time said, 'It would be interesting to fight beside you.'

Martel said, 'Haiti could use a man like you. You really ought to be an officer in the gendarmerie.'

Scarron smiled; another day, McAllister too might have enjoyed the joke.

'A beautiful morning,' Martel said. 'I wonder if the rains are over. Too early for the Christmas winds. Time for a clairin, hey?'

McAllister said, 'Not before breakfast, thank you. Maybe after work.'   ‒

Their breakfast was hot and they took it without much talk. The chicken was richly spiced, but what with his pain and impatience, and the naked Faustine serving them, McAllister could scarcely swallow; he gulped his coffee gratefully. He was breathing quicker, as he did before any action, and he did not deceive himself: it was a murderer's rapture rising in him, the emotion that would impel a decent man to the final and irrevocable breach of decency, horribly mingled with a final and irrevocable joy. But he did not like killing from ambush, and the coffee soured on his tongue.

He saw his friend the crone. They exchanged a nod. McAllister could not be comfortable among these people but could not dislike them. Martel offered cigarillos; his guests declined; the guerrilla smoked in the shade of a mountain mango tree. To quiet himself and to pass time McAllister said, 'What would you do if the Americans left?'

'Conquer,' Martel said, 'and rule. Look at Haiti: a happy, busy, pastoral people bustling about their daily work.' Deux Rochers was already torpid, and Martel's irony was more than broad – it was bitter. 'My God, what history has done to them!'

'History and their own masters,' Scarron said.

'Agreed, agreed,' Martel said. 'I suppose after a century we should stop blaming the blancs. When I first came to this village last year there was not even a faded memory of blancs: only legends. The blancs had constructed great palaces of wood and stone, I was told, and the blood of dead slaves thickened the mortar, slaves imported from Guinea and Dahomey, and some of these villagers

214

believe they are still in Guinea or Dahomey. They might as well be.'

McAllister said, 'The small people from the east, who are they? And why is there a charm against sandstorms?'

'Survivals of Africa,' Scarron said.

'There is a chant,' Martel said. '"The sun rises in the east, and sets in Guinea."'

'Old magic,' McAllister said.

Martel shrugged, and smoked, and said, 'You see magic as hocus-pocus. To my people the other world is real, and this daily life merely a pastime.'

'And to you?'

'The revolution is my god,' Martel said. 'But I wear a ouanga bag.'

'Revolution,' McAllister said. 'What's wrong with elections? We supervised a plebiscite last year and gave you a new constitution.'

Martel said, 'Merde, alors.'

'It was a farce,' Scarron said. 'The only clause so far invoked allows foreigners to own land. The rest is either irrelevant or unenforceable.'

'Good intentions,' McAllister said. 'The longer I stay the less I know.'

'Good intentions,' Martel said. 'I believed in them once, and I can remember the day I ceased to believe.' He flicked his cigarillo viciously into the fire, and asked Scarron, 'Do you remember?'

'I remember.'

'We were in school together,' Martel said, 'and one day, sitting among the priests, leafing through my history, I came across the account of an enlightened European, travelling through Haiti in seventeen-ninety. He was a gentle man and a friend to the poor Negro.'

A homily. A lecture. McAllister frowned; resentment stirred. This was not a time to discuss morals and manners.

'And in his account was the passage that told me who I was. I read it several times that day and never lost it. In the morning I speak it aloud as Ti-Jean prays to Christ. I carried it with me in France and Port-au-Prince and Cap-Haïtien and prison, and I carry it with me now, and I have never before spoken it aloud to a blanc but here it is.' Martel's eyes had reddened. He spoke swiftly in a cold, vindictive tone.

Scarron translated: '"A woman I saw, a young woman, one of the most beautiful women on the island, gave a banquet. Furious when a platter of botched pastries was served, she ordered her black cook seized and had him flung into the red-hot oven."'

McAllister muttered, 'Jesus.'

Martel said, 'The blancs used to stuff gunpowder up a black arse and blow a slave to bits, for amusement or example.'

After a moment McAllister said, 'Times change,' and immediately felt like a fool.

'Not unless we change them,' Martel said. 'You fear revolution, do you? But do you know what is the real wonder? Not the ferocity of a revolution,

216

when the brutes finally rise in a brief violent spasm, but their endless patient moderation.'

There seemed no answer to that; McAllister made none.

Soon Scarron said, 'Sufficient unto the day. Our problem is Blanchard.'

Martel said, 'Yes. In a war we must survive our enemies; in a revolution we must survive our friends.'

Blanchard said, 'Look there.'

A couple of acres of cane, and the stupefied marchers again, the chanting foreman with a bundle, the drugged labourers in lockstep. The men halted, the foreman passed machetes, they all vanished into the cane.

'It's two worlds,' he said. 'They march along like we weren't here, and we ride along like they weren't there.'

'I'm from another world too,' Caroline said.

'It was a mistake,' Blanchard said. 'I'd do it different now.'

'There's still time.' The heat fierce, still no breeze, and those ghastly slaves.

'I'll take care of you,' he said.

A runner: McAllister held his breath.

'About an hour,' Martel said. 'We'll ride on down.'

They saw Father Scarron wake with a start; he had dozed.

They rose, and slapped the dust away. Figures swayed to life near the huts; children gawked. McAllister removed his lieutenant's silver bars; they were all he wore that glinted.

Martel said, 'Not you, Ti-Jean. Stay here in the village.'

'The man is a Catholic?'

Martel shrugged. 'I believe so. He can have his last rites post mortem.'

'I'll go with you,' Scarron said.

'Not in white, please,' McAllister said. 'You can see white moving through the brush for miles. Start down when you hear the shot.'

'Hubert, Oreste, Pascal, Josius!' Martel's men fell in line. Guerrillas gathered to approve, to wish them luck, to inspect McAllister. Villagers peered from their huts.

On the fringe of the crowd Faustine loitered, half-naked. McAllister wondered: did she know? God, let Caroline be whole!

'Well, I am no use now,' Scarron said.

'You've done your job,' McAllister said.

'No pity? No mercy? Just hide behind a bush and shoot him?'

'Don't be sentimental,' McAllister said.

Martel said, 'Mercy is Ti-Jean's job.'

'No, it's God's,' Scarron said. 'Father Scarron cannot ask him to bless you. But Ti-Jean wishes you luck.'

* * *

'Let's just sniff the morning,' Blanchard said. 'No hurry.' They paused beneath a tall gnarled bougainvillaea all in red flower.

'Shade,' Caroline said, 'Thank God.'

The earth was a dull green everywhere, only brighter on the broadleaves, and the sky was a remote cloudless blue. A rich hot hairy smell rose, of horse and mule; from the profusion of blossom above her, a single scarlet flower floated down.

'Take some water,' he said. 'Soon be home. Down to that stream, across, a mile up the hill.'

Home. She drank. Her sweaty clothes stung, her head itched, her heart was cold and closed.

'I suppose I'm sorry,' he said. He coughed once, and wiped his lips on his sleeve. 'Quiet. Dead time of day. Let's move.'

They rode across the last mile side by side. When two black figures rose from the brush, advanced to the far bank and waved, Blanchard said, 'That's better. Josius, and Oreste. Good men. Good fighters. They stand fast. You need men who stand fast.'

On the shallow bank Caroline's mule refused the water, then lurched forward to bury his nose and drink. She hauled back sharply on the halter, and Blanchard leaned across to swat him on the rump. The mule edged into the stream, and Sammy beside him.

McAllister lay prone within a dense mass of brush and oleander. He was hatless, he had a clear view of the approach and the ford, and when he saw Caroline he thanked God, and snugged the butt to his shoulder. The rifle was an old friend, an Enfield, with tiny ears to protect the front sight and an aperture rear sight. No fancy shooting today. There were five cartridges in the clip and one bull's-eye would do it. The two Haitians stood on the bank and called greetings and encouragement. Martel was some yards to McAllister's left, and the horses were uphill, feeding and therefore quiet. The sun rode high.

McAllister sighted on the centre of Blanchard's chest. The front sight bobbed and wove infinitesimally; he breathed, again, willed his muscles calm. Caroline was this side of Blanchard but the angle was sufficient. They were fifty yards from him, and he let them come on, and held the front sight on Blanchard's chest. McAllister was wholly concentrated: he had seen from a distance that Blanchard wore a sombrero and rode a superb horse, but all that mattered now was the bull's-eye.

Blanchard coughed, and hunched away from the front sight. McAllister took his time. Caroline leaned to Blanchard and laid a hand on his shoulder. McAllister let his eyes flit to her and was shaken: she was murmuring to Blanchard, concerned, a half smile.

He sighted finer, and pressed the trigger lightly, preparing; he filled his lungs, exhaled briefly, held his breath, Blanchard coughed again and bent forward. This was McAllister's vocation and his rifle was steady, but he committed simple human error, and glanced at the man's face. It leapt at him, familiar, angry, the blue eyes not dead but pained: yes, the cough, the moustache, the distant echo, the great war, a cold day, a hill, an abbey – where? when? Fire now, you fool!

When Blanchard contracted, coughing, Caroline said, 'Hold on. Almost home.' She saw blood on his lips and remembered that he had kissed her, and sadly she watched him writhe. He heaved himself up in the saddle to draw a huge breath, he spat a great gob of blood, and there was an immense explosion. Caroline was dazed. McAllister called her name, and she sat stupefied.

McAllister pulled his shot, jolted his aim off true: the face from another world, his own startled twitch, Blanchard rising in the stirrups: McAllister caught him in the ribs, low and to the left, and was so surprised that he forgot to work the bolt, only gaped and wondered – for a second, two, but it was enough. He sprang to his feet, and worked the bolt and shouted, 'Caroline!'

Martel saw Blanchard rise and twist, and fall against the woman, almost before he heard the shot. He vaulted from his screen of brush shouting, 'For Fleury! For Fleury, you son of a bitch!' and stood flourishing his bullwhip, massive and exultant and happy, freed of this blanc at last! 'For Fleury and for Haiti!'

Blanchard slumped to his left; his right hand went to the scabbard and yanked at the rifle; he fell against warm flesh, the woman was shrieking, 'No!' Down, he dragged her down, his foot was free and he was resting on the woman's body and fumbling for the bolt, the trigger, the safety, but he could not see, the sky had darkened. He took in a great breath, and bubbled; he lay across warm flesh in the shallows and he embraced the rifle.

Light returned; a vast blue sky glowed above him. He saw Martel, the huge man, the gleaming grin. And he saw the blanc, the rifleman. For one instant of pure serenity Blanchard's earth stood still; he sighted; he fired.

Caroline struggled free, shouting again, 'No! Bobby, no!' Blanchard rolled on to his back and lay still, eyes open; his blood oozed into the stream. 'No, no, no!' she shouted over and over, and tore at Blanchard's shirt, a bandage, the wound was bad; intact, the ouanga bag lay on a crimson pulp; and when an arm came around her shoulders she flung it off. 'Down!' It was Bobby shouting at her; he grasped her by the upper arm, tugged her off Blanchard and shoved her flat.

Blanchard wheezed faintly. His rifle lay under-water, and his hand clutched it still. He worked to keep the sky blue. It dimmed to grey, flared once more to blue. He was bruised; he ached with every breath.

McAllister had seen Blanchard take wavering aim and had charged forward; heard the shot and seen Blanchard flop, drop the weapon, go limp; charged on, grappled Caroline down. She struggled and shouted, a savage scream, and then she was beating at him, jabbing at his face, whacking, backhanding, shrieking, 'You! You!' Christ, the poor hysterical creature! He pinned her wrists, scanned the bank, glimpsed the fallen Martel. Caroline wailed. He slapped her once, hard, and roared, 'You're all right! Blanchard's dead!'

She fell slack in his arms; she sobbed, and was still.

'He's not dead,' Blanchard breathed.

'Blanchard!' Caroline cried. 'Let me see.' She tore herself free.

Blanchard closed his eyes and blew little pink bubbles; the sun struck rainbows from his lips.

McAllister knelt. 'Blanchard. Can you hear me? You missed, man, you missed your aim. You've shot Martel.'

Blanchard strained for air, for the strength to speak. 'Missed, hell.' His face twisted, a flicker of memory, recognition. He whispered hoarsely, 'Seen you before. Tin soldier.' Then angrily: 'Something wrong here.' In a queer strangled rattle he gasped, 'I know you.' His hand rose from the water, and wavered towards Caroline, and he died.

McAllister sprinted. He pushed his way between Haitians. 'Martel! Where's the wound?'

'In the belly.' Martel's breathing was shallow, his eyes were dull. 'My own fault. For once I let myself be happy. Is he dead?'

'Yes. Dead.'

'I thank God for that.' The black face paled: granite.

Caroline sat limp in the shallows, watching the gentle eddies suck Blanchard's blood away. She heard McAllister call, and did not care. She heard his step, his voice: 'Martel's alive. Not for long.' She rose obediently and followed him. He said no more; nor did he touch her.

She knelt beside the guerrilla. His wound was neat.

He panted gently. 'You are Mam'selle Barbour?'

She nodded.

'Speak up,' he said. 'I can't see.'

'Yes,' she said.

'Ravi,' he said. His eyes searched for something far beyond her.

She accepted McAllister's bandanna, folded it in four, and pressed it carefully to the wound. She shook her head, rose, and returned to Blanchard's corpse.

* * *

Scarron arrived shortly, with an escort, two mounted Cacos. McAllister reported; he and the priest went directly to Martel. 'Charlot.'

Martel opened his eyes. 'Judas. Well, you have your blanche.'

'And you have your blanc, if it's any comfort.'

'It is, it is.' For a moment Martel was almost jolly. 'Bring him here. Here beside me.'

Scarron nodded to McAllister.

The stream gurgled; Sammy and the mule had watered and now wandered on to the bank. The faint rustle and flow of forest and stream only deepened the hot silence. McAllister took Caroline's hand and urged her ashore. She was kneeling in the shallows and said, 'Not yet.'

He slung his rifle, squatted on the bank beside her and turned her face towards his. He gazed at her for some time, and she at him, and he decided to say nothing. He touched her cheek, her forehead.

She closed Blanchard's eyes, and freed the ouanga bag. She slipped the rawhide over her own head, and freed her hair. The ouanga bag nestled between her breasts. McAllister salvaged the man's weapons, laid them against a bush ashore, and hauled on the body. Caroline followed him.

'Lay him here,' Martel whispered, and they stretched Blanchard beside him. Martel turned his head, and peered. 'Salaud.' With effort, he spat

225

towards the dead man; the thin spittle lay on his own cheek and chin. 'Ti-Jean,' he said, 'I had best have the last rites. I feel better now, but just in case.'

McAllister asked, 'Shall we take you in? There are good doctors, and a military hospital.'

'I think not,' Martel said.

The villagers were arriving, women and children, armed men, trudging out of the forest and on to the broad bank. They paused, and some knelt, seeing Father Scarron at work; others gawked at the dead blanc, the living blanc, the mournful blanche. Scarron daubed the two men, one dead, one dying, with holy oils from his little black bag; he murmured Latin. When he said, '. . . deliquesti, Amen,' forty voices repeated, 'Amen,' and he sent the two rebels to eternity in the name of the Father and the Son and the Holy Ghost. The villagers stood in clumps then; some murmured to Martel. McAllister saw Faustine, who showed no emotion; he resisted the impulse to point her out. The Haitians crossed themselves and wailed. Oreste cried out fiercely, and bent to mutter.

Martel said, 'No. I gave my word.'

Father Scarron embraced Caroline, and she clung to him. 'We had best leave,' he said.

McAllister bowed his head in sudden desolation: we who are about to die salute you. He marched up the trail a little way, half expecting to find no

226

horse: but there stood his mount, tethered and cropping, beside Martel's. He mounted and rode back to the stream. He kept his mind on his work: Blanchard's horse for Caroline, the mule of no importance. Take Blanchard's body in? Would the Cacos make a move?

'Bobby.' She was at the stream, where Blanchard had lain.

'Caroline, listen — '

'Come here.'

The stream flowed, placid, clear. Caroline sat on the bank, the empty ouanga bag in one hand. She showed him the other. 'This was all.'

A small silver cross, with a lion standing on a crown, the cross dangling from a crimson ribbon; and the small crimson medal, tiny lion, tiny crown on the cross centred, for everyday wear.

Well up the bank, almost in the forest, shielding Martel and Blanchard, the ranks of Cacos and sullen villagers stood, in motley or cotton or half-naked, leaden now and stunned. McAllister saw round faces, long faces, bald women, surly pot-bellied men, naked children shoving and giggling. The Haitians were watching the priest and his two friends. Voices rose, others hushed them.

Time to leave.

McAllister took Caroline's hand for a moment only.

'You killed him,' Caroline said.

'Yes, and would again.' He spoke sharper than he wanted.

'From ambush.'

'Did you want a hero? You know who I am.' He stood taller, unyielding. 'He did his dirty job and I did mine. He was a killer.'

'Oh he was, he was!'

'Leave him in peace,' Scarron said. 'The soul has departed.'

Caroline stepped to Blanchard's horse and said, 'Come on, Sammy.'

McAllister said, 'Sammy?'

Blanchard's rifle was in its scabbard, the slaughtering knife in its sheath, the pistol belt looped over the high pommel. Caroline grasped the belt, and McAllister said, 'I'll take that.'

'I'll wear it,' she said. 'I'll keep the knife too. It was his father's.'

McAllister let his hand drop. He checked his own tack, his rifle. He waited for Caroline to mount, and when she was up he saw her eyes moist.

'You never said a Mass,' he reminded Scarron.

'Another time,' the priest said.

'Good. Caroline: I knew him too.'

'You knew him too,' she said slowly.

'He wasn't French at all,' McAllister said. 'He was British.'

Caroline said, 'No. He was not.'

McAllister was perplexed and curious, but eased off again. He drew his silver bars from a pocket and pinned them to his collar. 'There. No sense careering around the countryside like a bandit. We have much to talk about, my love. When you're ready.' He drew back. 'You two wait here.'

Within a ring of fifty Haitians, he stood over Martel, who lay like an effigy, a brooding stone idol overthrown, huge and helpless. 'Goodbye, big man.'

'Goodbye, Lieutenant. You'll lose. You know that. In the end you'll lose.'

'The end,' McAllister said. 'That's a long way down the road.'

'Not for me,' Martel said. 'Move out now, while I am still their leader.'

McAllister waved a salute, and turned away.

'I'll tow the mule and hang back a bit, just to keep an eye on these folks. All right, Caroline? Lead on, Father.'

Once more into the ford, and a score of rifles behind him on the bank, and his back a mile wide; the stream purling, the vast green plain beyond the farther shore. Against all instinct he turned in the saddle; he halted his mount and raised a sad hand in farewell. No one stirred, not even a child, and that was the last he saw of them: a grieving dark crowd of half-naked natives, among whom he had lived for a day and a night.

* * *

They travelled slowly, and Caroline said not a word. In an hour or so they heard tambours beating slowly. At another stream Caroline bathed, and washed her clothes and wriggled into the wet garments; they cooled her. She had restored the medals to Blanchard's ouanga bag and was wearing it. That night they camped quietly, like mourners or pilgrims, and he dished up rations. 'We'll stand watch,' he said to Scarron. 'I'll wake you in four hours or so.' And to Caroline, 'Sleep. Will you take a cup of rum?'

She did, and he only said, 'Good night now.' And in the morning he only said, 'Good morning,' but when Scarron said, 'Top o' the morning,' she smiled hazily; more, she was famished.

They rode, and took shelter from the noonday sun, and all day the tambours followed them. In midafternoon the breeze revived, and McAllister rode beside Caroline. Her hair was tangled and her shirt and trousers were wrinkled and stained, but her beauty would never fade, he knew that, not for him, so he said, 'We should be married when your father arrives. All's well that ends well.'

'My father?'

'He's aboard a battle wagon now. Back in the real world, remember?'

'The real world. Ah,' she groaned, 'ah, I did something terrible.'

He waited, and when she said no more he

answered: 'I doubt that, and I don't believe I'd care.'

'I have not excelled,' she said.

'You sure talk funny. Maybe you need a husband. Homely but honest.'

'I have not excelled in virtue,' she said.

'That's good news,' McAllister said. 'You excel in other respects, and I'll just have to put up with your vices. Do you want to cry?'

'I don't need to cry,' she said.

'Splendid woman,' he said. 'I do, now and then. It is sometimes the only reasonable reaction to life.'

'I'll think about it,' she said. The sun was setting before them, vast sheets of orange fading to yellow, and little humped green hills dimming to purple on the horizon.

'There's another reasonable reaction,' he said. 'It's a long life sentence and what else is worth it but love?'

Father Scarron, behind them, called, 'I can hear every word.'

So they rode on, and shortly they made camp again, not far now, home to Hinche in the morning. And over their evening meal Father Scarron said, 'He called me Judas.'

McAllister said, 'Of course. We all like to make much of ourselves.'

'Damn you for a shrewd one,' Scarron said. 'You're older.'

They ate and drank, and drank again beneath

the yellow moon and the scatter of stars, and then the priest said, 'Do you know, once upon a time the bride and groom had to promise, "With my body I thee worship." It is a good answer to death, though perhaps a priest should not say so.'

As the last light faded Caroline walked a little way apart, to be by herself. McAllister cleaned up their leavings, and scrubbed the mess kits with sandy dirt. 'Wise, wise you are,' Scarron said. 'Give her all the time she needs.'

'I don't care if she never tells me,' McAllister said, 'but she has to let it out before it kills her.'

Later Caroline stood before McAllister and said, 'Lieutenant, if you will take me away from all this I promise to be very good to you.'

'I'll think about it,' he said, and he seemed to hear their hearts beating like tambours.

'Bobby,' she said, 'I'm going to cry now. I'm not pretty when I cry.'

'I don't want a pretty woman,' he said. 'They always ask for jewellery. I want a good crier. Come here.'

They had not ridden for an hour in the morning when they saw dust, and a small column that broke into a gallop. The breeze had held, and the three jogged along in comfort, sun at their backs, and the column raced towards them. It proved to be Dillingham with a squad, hooting and hollering and raising a cheer when they were sure it was a woman.

Dillingham almost skidded to a halt. Flanagan circled the group, uttering war whoops and urging his horse to prance and rear, against all regulations. Dillingham's eyes were shining: 'Miss Barbour! Miss Barbour, respects from the whole camp. Mac – we heard! Never saw such a happy mob of leatherheads! Father Scarron: thank you, Father. We all thank you.'

McAllister said, 'You heard? How'd you hear?'

'Lafayette,' Dillingham said. 'How else?' The mounted men had surrounded them, and were grinning and touching their hats to Caroline. Dillingham went on: 'They're both dead?'

'The white Caco for sure. Martel with a bullet in the belly.'

The squad raised a wild, shrill cheer, and the men shouted praise. But McAllister was not laughing, and Caroline and Father Scarron had not spoken. The cheering died, the grins faded, respectful solemnity prevailed.

Dillingham asked, 'You all right, Mac?'

'I'm just fine. Just aged a bit.'

'Then it wasn't easy.'

'We're all tired,' McAllister said.

'Sure you are,' Dillingham said. 'Do you need food? Drink?'

McAllister said, 'We'll wait.'

'Flanagan! Over here!' And to Caroline: 'Do you need a doctor, Miss?'

'No, thank you, Lieutenant.'

'Flanagan – back to camp and report! All ship-

233

shape, no doctor. Flank speed, man! Captain Healy give you a cigar!'

Flanagan yelped again and cantered off.

'Well, by God, Mac, by God, Mac, by God.'

As the three rode among their escort Caroline said sadly, 'They're like schoolboys.'

McAllister said, 'No, they're men, and some of them will die badly and they all know that. Beware pride, Miss.'

They entered the camp at Hinche to a festival welcome: a couple of hundred Marines cheering their lungs out, and volley after volley of blanks from a squad of riflemen, and Healy on the veranda waving, and Lafayette darting out to toss a flower amid roars from the ranks. The Marines stood before their tents in ironed khakis, and the company streets were like ruled lines, and had been policed: not a scrap of paper, not a cigarette butt. McAllister imagined the morning's work, the men darning, mending, blacking, oiling, spitting and polishing boots and buckles; he imagined the inspection. Their campaign hats sat square and flat-brimmed; no cowboys today. Captain Healy shouted, 'Hats off!' and off they came, and the men waved them and shouted.

Caroline said, 'No band.'

'Stop that,' McAllister said. 'They care.'

Scarron said, 'That's the hell of it. They do care.'

They rode to the veranda and dismounted to

more cheers. Captain Healy marched down the steps and said, 'Miss Barbour, I hope you're as happy as I am. Can't remember a day like this. Healy, Miss, captain, at your service.'

'Yes,' she said. 'Yes, thank you, Captain Healy, of course I'm happy. I'm so grateful.'

'Well, it was all McAllister here. No doing anything with these romantic young fellows. Miss, I'm making jokes because I don't know how to say how glad I am. I trust you're well.'

'Yes. I'm well.'

Dillingham stood beaming beside his captain.

'And Father Scarron: the Corps owes you a debt. You can do me one more favour and say grace at dinner tonight. Colonel probably fly up this afternoon. I'm giving the men all sorts of leave and privileges. Cancelled all punishment, by golly. It is a holiday and an occasion for thanksgiving.'

'Delighted,' said Father Scarron.

'Come up on the veranda now and let the men have a look at you. Here you go, Miss Barbour.'

They flowed up the steps in a body, and the cheering resumed. Healy asked, 'Mac, was he American?'

McAllister said, 'No sir.'

'By God, I'm glad of that. There you go, Miss Barbour. Safe and sound now, and among friends, and your father will hear the news at sea. Now then: line up along the rail.' Healy waved to his overjoyed troops, who roared back at him and shattered the heavens with rebel yells. 'Speak up,

Miss Caroline. Got to talk pretty or I'll have a mutiny on my hands.' He raised those hands for silence.

Caroline glanced wildly at McAllister, who showed amusement. 'You've been through worse. And you look sweet wearing a pistol.'

'Oh dear God,' she muttered. She stood taller, between McAllister and Scarron, and called out, 'Men!'

They cheered again, whistled, yipped.

Caroline laid a hand on the ouanga bag. All these men in khaki. Blanchard's sombrero, and that one lovely smile — where was his sombrero? Bobbing downstream. She drew a long breath, and heard herself tell these men that she knew a bit of what they faced, and was proud to be the daughter of a Marine.

Pandemonium. At the edge of camp the Haitian vendors shouted and danced.

Healy called for silence. In time he had it. 'You men! This is Father Jean-Baptiste Scarron and without him it would not have happened. Let's hear some thanks!'

Lesser pandemonium; no ill will; one cry of 'Up the Pope!'

Scarron waved modestly, a blessing, two fingers.

Caroline said, 'I suppose they're buried by now.'

Scarron said, 'No. The villagers will burn them tonight, side by side, on a great pyre, and there will be chanting, and keening.'

Caroline said, 'God keep them. I'm still . . . out there. I can't believe it's over.'

'It's over,' McAllister said. 'You're back from Haiti.'

Scarron said, 'It's not over for me. I'm not back from Haiti.'

Captain Healy burst among them with a monstrous great grin, and waved a cigar; he flung an arm across McAllister's shoulders and shouted over the cheering, 'By God, Mac! There's a medal in this for you — bound to be!'

The world's greatest novelists now available in paperback from Grafton Books

Eric van Lustbader

Jian	£3.50 ☐
The Miko	£2.95 ☐
The Ninja	£3.50 ☐
Sirens	£3.50 ☐
Beneath An Opal Moon	£2.95 ☐
Black Heart	£3.50 ☐

Nelson de Mille

By the Rivers of Babylon	£2.50 ☐
Cathedral	£1.95 ☐
The Talbot Odyssey	£3.50 ☐

Justin Scott

The Shipkiller	£2.50 ☐
The Man Who Loved the Normandie	£2.50 ☐
A Pride of Kings	£2.95 ☐

Leslie Waller

Trocadero	£2.50 ☐
The Swiss Account	£2.50 ☐
The American	£2.50 ☐
The Family	£1.95 ☐
The Banker	£2.50 ☐
The Brave and the Free	£1.95 ☐
Gameplan	£1.95 ☐

David Charney

Sensei	£2.50 ☐
Sensei II: The Swordmaster	£2.50 ☐

Paul-Loup Sulitzer

The Green King	£2.95 ☐

To order direct from the publisher just tick the titles you want
and fill in the order form.

All these books are available at your local bookshop or newsagent, or can be ordered direct from the publisher.

To order direct from the publishers just tick the titles you want and fill in the form below.

Name _____

Address _____

_____

Send to:
Grafton Cash Sales
PO Box 11, Falmouth, Cornwall TR10 9EN.

Please enclose remittance to the value of the cover price plus:

UK 60p for the first book, 25p for the second book plus 15p per copy for each additional book ordered to a maximum charge of £1.90.

BFPO 60p for the first book, 25p for the second book plus 15p per copy for the next 7 books, thereafter 9p per book.

Overseas including Eire £1.25 for the first book, 75p for second book and 28p for each additional book.